CHAPTER ONE

It is a filthy, supposedly spring day, in a North Cornish market town. The river, the Camel, is brown and dangerously high; there has been so much rain. Umbrellas, beige, navy, tug furiously at their owners who want to stop and gossip outside the Coop.

It is still early in the year, the weather March- wild, and only a handful of hardy visitors mingle with the scurrying local shoppers. They mooch, damp and disenchanted around the small town centre where most of the gift shops are preparing for- weather permitting, and it so often doesn't- the holiday season.

None of them notice, and why should they? A little girl, about nine years old is standing looking up, her little face creased with anxiety, at the woman who stands motionless beside her, seemingly gazing at the shop window.

However, the woman sees nothing. Neither is she hearing anything, not the traffic as it rumbles along the main street behind her, or even her granddaughter who has her hand on her arm and is desperately trying to get her attention.

The woman's' grandson, soon to be seven, is scuffing his shoes on a lampost, and clutching his new toy plane, still wrapped, the idea of which no longer holds his interest.

"Why are we still here" he whines. "I'm bored. It's boring standing here. I'm...."

"Shut up George," his sister flashes at him. Then in a hushed tone. "I don't know what Granny's looking at."

The little girl looks down at her feet, thn across the street, then back to her grandmother. She tugs gently at her coat sleeve.

"Granny. Granny, can we go now? George is going to start making a real fuss in a minute, and I'm a bit thirsty. But I can wait 'till we get home," she adds quickly, thoughtfully. Granny doesn't have much money, Mum said, and Lizzie knows that drinks 'bought out' were expensive. Lizzie loves her grandmother, and she is at a loss. Granny has never, ever done this before, not stopped dead in front of a shop window, and just stayed there. She hasn't said anything either, not since they stopped – not one word. Usually Granny was always talking to her and George, chatting away, asking them things.

Another long minute goes by.

"I'm going back to the car," George announces crossly, staring at his grandmother, hoping to put into her head the idea of the busy road he would have to cross, not that he really dared, to get back to the library car park. "Granny". He is really whining now. "Come on Granny. Let's go. This is boring."

Mrs du Bois' bag starts to vibrate – her mobile phone is ringing. Both children look expectantly from their grandmother to the handbag dangling from her shoulder. She must be able to feel it surely, must have heard it buzzing but she is making no move to open her bag and answer it.

"Granny – your phone." Lizzie puts a hand on the bag opening, and meeting no resistance, takes the phone out and presses the green button.

"Hello. Llo." A confused little catch enters her voice, a catch, then a wobble. "Mummy? Mum" she breathes tremulously, glancing up at her grandmother.

By now, George is swinging round and round the lamppost muttering to himself. Lizzie, big-eyed, and holding the phone tightly, hisses at her brother.

"George! The cars. Stop doing that. Mum, George is swinging round, right by the traffic...I have told him....George, Mum says you've got to stop, stand still....Granny? She's looking in this shop window.... Granny, Mum wants to speak to you."

THREADS

CAROLINE HIBBERT

authorHOUSE

AuthorHouse™ UK
1663 Liberty Drive
Bloomington, IN 47403 USA
www.authorhouse.co.uk
Phone: UK TFN: 0800 0148641 (Toll Free inside the UK)
UK Local: (02) 0369 56322 (+44 20 3695 6322 from outside the UK)

© 2024 Caroline Hibbert. All rights reserved.

No part of this book may be reproduced, stored in a retrieval system, or transmitted by any means without the written permission of the author.

Published by AuthorHouse 03/26/2024

ISBN: 979-8-8230-8716-2 (sc)
ISBN: 979-8-8230-8718-6 (hc)
ISBN: 979-8-8230-8717-9 (e)

Library of Congress Control Number: 2024906333

Print information available on the last page.

Any people depicted in stock imagery provided by Getty Images are models, and such images are being used for illustrative purposes only.
Certain stock imagery © Getty Images.

This book is printed on acid-free paper.

Because of the dynamic nature of the Internet, any web addresses or links contained in this book may have changed since publication and may no longer be valid. The views expressed in this work are solely those of the author and do not necessarily reflect the views of the publisher, and the publisher hereby disclaims any responsibility for them.

BRIEF SUMMARY

This is a contemporary novel set in late 20th century London and Cornwall based on a theme of 'Sins of the Fathers', which tells of the effect one man's perverted instincts has on his family.

As the main characters reach adulthood, threads of memory finally backed up through the ensuing years, by irrefutable evidence, reveal that their lives had been thwarted from birth and any chance of happiness had been stolen, rendering all their efforts and aspirations useless.

As the secrets spill out, Anna and Lucy, unable to withstand these truths, slip over the edges of sanity into the only bearable reality left to them.

SYNOPSIS

Anna has had a reasonable upbringing by her divorced mother. She goes on to have children and grandchildren, but this cannot protect her from the emerging truths.

Lucy whose childhood was blighted, marries Nigel who grew up just down the road in Sycamore Avenue. Neither Lucy, who is so close to the truth she cannot see it, nor Nigel, brought up by his single mother and maternal grandparents, simply never wonders, just like his father, never looks inside himself.

The story moves back and forth through time and the lives of these three innocents.

Lizzie holds the phone out towards her grandmother, but her grandmother doesn't even turn her head.

"Granny. It's Mum, Mum, she won't take it. She won't take the phone. She's just standing here staring at the window. We've been here ages." Lizzie's face begins to crumple. She is trying her hardest not to cry. She takes a big gulp of air. "Mum, can you come? Now? Now she smiles a fragile, reassured smile. "Yes, we'll wait....Yes, in the library car park.....Yes, by the art shop....Yes, we will...Yes. Bye"

"George," Lizzie speaks as sternly as she can manage, to her brother. She already realizes that there is no point in even trying to speak to her grandmother. "Mum's coming to get us. We've got to wait here."

George stops in mid-swing, dropping his package which he has been clutching under his arm, and, dizzy from his circling of the lamppost, stumbles and steps down hard on his present.

"Oh" he starts to wail. "Look! Now I've broken my plane, and I haven't even unwrapped it yet. Why can't Granny take us home? Why's Mum coming? I thought we were going back to Grannies' I wanted to watch her old Black Knight video. Oh!"

George crouches down and picks up the remnants of his plane, still neatly wrapped in its' shop bag, but now making ominously crackly, broken noises. George stands, crying now, glaring accusingly up at his grandmother, and then, with more frightened eyes, at Lizzie. Lizzie pulls him towards her, and hangs onto his arm. She tucks the mobile phone back into her grandmothers' bag, and holds onto her too, just lightly by the hand. Her grandmothers' hand is ice-cold, and hanging limply at her side. She doesn't clutch Lizzie's in warm response as she normally would. Usually she would squeeze Lzzie's hand tight, and probably give her a big hug into the bargain. Granny did a lot of that, hugging and cuddling – usually.

It begins to rain quite hard, as the three of them stand on the pavement close together, arms linked, though in the case of Anna du Bois, hopelessly and irretrievably disconnected, waiting to be rescued.

CHAPTER TWO

"We've got to go to Bodmin, to the hospital......No, no-one's had an accident.....It's not like that. It's Mum.....No, she's not hurt, least I don't think so......It was really weird Em. I'll tell you all about it later... Yesterday?...... I couldn't get you, could I? ...... I did keep trying, course I did, and then I thought I may as well leave it 'till the morning........ Yes, I know, but what could you have done?......Yes, about two..... You wouldn't have time to be there before that anyway.... No rush now – she isn't going anywhere......Yes, she is........ No, don't worry....Yes, see you later. Got to drop the kids off first.... Bye."

Jenny puts the phone down and goes to the foot of the stairs, calls up. "Come on you two – time to go to your Dads."

Lizzie appears first, hair neatly brushed. "But what about Granny, Mum?"

"Don't you worry about Granny. Auntie Em and I are going to see her, see what's going on. She'll be fine, don't you worry. The people who are looking after her are brilliant. She'll have them falling about in the aisles in no time. When she gets back to her old self. You know what she's like." Jen shouts now. "George, hurry up. Wash your face, and make sure your shorts are clean."

"Can't I come – to see Granny, I mean?" Lizzie asks, her beautiful childs face scrunched up in concern.

"Don't frown like that." Jenny snaps. "You'll have frown lines before you're ten, miss. No, you go to Dads, and when Granny's better....."

"But when will that be?" Lizzies big grey eyes fill with tears. Jenny, her hand flexing on the newel post feels her heart shift at the sight of her beautiful daughter's scrunched up face. Trevor was a fool. Why wasn't he here for Lizzie, for herself, for all of them? How could he exist, not seeing his lovely Lizzie every day?

"I don't know darling – honestly. We'll just have to wait and see. Now stop your worrying, and go and drag that wretched brother of yours out of his bedroom please. Make a pit stop in the bathroom, and chuck a flannel at him, while you're at it."

Lizzie smiles, a watery sunny smile, then giggles wickedly as she steps backwards up the stairs, leaning her weight on one arm on the bannistair, and the other on the wall which is already well marked by small fingers.

The sisters arrive simultaneously, swinging into the hospital car park Emma raises a hand as they manage to park opposite one another. She is out of her car, and opening Jenny's door while Jenny is still reaching into the back for her handbag. She notes with annoyance, the preoccupied look on Jenny's face.

"Well, come on, tell me. What happened? I've only been away twenty four hours, and I spoke to Mum yesterday morning." Emma gabbles, her voice rising.

Jenny gets out of the car, and fiddles with her keys as she tries to lock the door.

"How was France?"

Emmas' face is pink. "Never mind France, Jen. Where's Mum?. Is she in bed here, or what? Is she ill?"

"Calm down Em, for God's sake. Let me just get this damn thing locked. The central locking's gone all....."

"Jenny." Emma uncharacteristically raises her voice until it sounds almost rough. "Just tell me, for Christ's sake. What's going on? She sounded fine yesterday."

"Well" Jenny is fiddling with her keys, "She's not now." She glances at her sisters' anxious face. She places a hand on Emma's arm. "Oh Em, sorry. She is O.K. really. You'll see. She's seeing a Doctor this afternoon."

"A doctor? This afternoon? But she came here yesterday afternoon, didn't you say, and she hasn't been seen by a Doctor yet?"

Jenny squeezes Emma's arm.

"It's not that sort of thing, illness, apparently. The people I saw yesterday, nurses, and oh I don't know, a ward manager or something, I think he called himself, said she might have had some sort of breakdown. Anyway she's bound to have been seen by someone else by now. The doctor I spoke to this morning, a consultant or something, can't remember now, sounded as if he was God; he isn't seeing. Mum before three oclock, but he wanted us here about two."

The girls reach the parking machines. They fumble about for the right change, find it between them, and turn back to their cars

"Why does the doctor want to see us, and before he sees Mum? If he, God, as you call him, hasn't even seen her, he won't be able to tell us anything."

"No, but he might want to ask us a few things about Mum. Phew! Key actually worked this time. What's the matter?" Jenny is looking at Emma who is hesitating beside her car

"We should have come this morning, never mind what they said. I feel awful now. What if she's been waiting for us?"

"Don't be so daft." Jenny stashes her keys in her bag and swings it over her shoulder. If we'd come this morning, we'd have had to stay all day."

"Aw Jen".

"Don't look at me like that. I'm not being mean, but we can't come twice in one day – it's a thirty mile round trip – even further for me. And if we had been here all day, what could we have done anyway, just sat around staring at each other, no-one knowing what the hell was going on. There's bound to have been stuff to do, you know hospital routine and all that. Nothing to do with us. She probably hasn't had time to miss us. She'll be O.K."

"I suppose so. Poor old mum. Wonder what she thought when she woke up in here this morning"

"She woke up in here yesterday, well, sort of."

They reach the automatic doors. They step inside where the air conditioning cannot disguise the change in the smell in the air. Both girls shudder a little, blame the air conditioning. It is warm outside.

"You know what I mean. She wasn't really with it yesterday, when she came in here, was she?"

"No, but" Jenny peers up at the list of wards and floor numbers. She presses a button for the lift. "She sounded O.K. this morning, chatting away, almost as if she was at home."

Emma turns quickly. "Really? You phoned her this morning? Why didn't you say?"

"Well, you know, I had to phone to fix this appointment, so I asked to speak to her while I was at it."

"Oh" Emma sighs. "I wish I'd come earlier, last night."

"How could you – you weren't even in the country, you were halfway across the blooming channel."

"Wish we'd never gone. What was she like then, this morning?"

"Oh, bit vague, kept saying odd things, then forgetting my name, and where she was, then the next minute, she seemed quite normal." Heavens, sound a bit like me!

"I guess we've all got it lurking, especially in our family, waiting to pounce, dementia, - alzheimers."

The lift stops and the girls step out and Emma looks around for the right arrows.

"Don't be so melodramatic – course we havn't got it waiting to pounce" Jenny scoffs. "Old people forget things – fact of life. Their memory cells are all used up – full. You can't go on storing stuff indefinitely"

"Maybe it's not that with Mum. Maybe everything's just got to much for her, too much to deal with. Look, it's this way."

"What do you mean? She's just switched off? Huh! Must try that some time."

Emma looks sideways at Jenny, who carries on, oblivious to the effect of her words on her sister.

"She was certainly switched off yesterday, but listening to her this morning, something seems to have cranked her up again."

"Hardly up?" Emma snorts.

"You know what I mean. She was quite cheerful some of the time,

7

remembering and things, but you should have seen her yesterday, Em. It was awful –really scary."

"Frightening for the kids too."

"Yeah, exactly. Lizzie coped brilliantly, but we don't want that happening again."

Emma turns, as they reach swing doors "Do you think it's happened before – you know, at home? Gets over it, comes out of it, whatever, before anyone else sees, notices anything."

They have arrived in a reception area, but there is no-one in sight.

"Maybe" Jenny says Jenny vaguely, as she looks around for a person, a notice, some clue as to where to go. "Who knows?"

Emma sighs. "We could try asking her."

"Should let the doctors do that eh? They know the right things to ask, and presumably, the right way to ask them."

"We hope"

They stand looking at one another for a minute. No-one comes.

"Are we in the right place? You came here yesterday." Emma, eyebrows raised, looks at her sister..

"Well, it was a bit of a blur. Didn't recognize the car park bit, come to think of it. I think I must have come in a different entrance. We seem to have walked miles. Must be on the wrong wing or whatever. Let's go back to the lift – get our bearings." The two young women retrace their steps back to the lift.

"Look Psychiatric wards and way out. We've come the long way round".

Jenny buzzes for the lift and they go down four floors.

"Big place huh? Not like it used to be. Remember? Used to be ye olde cottage hospital." says Emma.

"Yeah, in the last century. This is it. Yes I remember that dreadful picture. Still it's a bit cheerier than up there." Jenny points in the air and wrinkles her nose. "This bit even smells better."

They come to a reception area. Emma asks for Valency ward. The receptionist points them in the right direction along a maze of wide shiny floored corridors. The two old hospitals in Bodmin have been replaced by this spanking new building. Everything is shiny and new. Pictures drawn by local school children adorn the corridor walls. Everywhere is light and airy, unlike the old buildings which were prehistoric by comparison, more like Victorian institutions which they probably had been, with their murky green and brown painted corridors and big, heavy, usually locked doors.

The girls, reach a dead end at glass doors which don't want to open.

Jenny peers through the glass.

"Hey Blimey! Come and look at this Em" She moves to one side pointing through the glass panes. "Bloomin' Florence Nightingale. Just look at that hat! And flowers, flowers everywhere. Different world eh? Must be the PP ward".

"What?" Emma says distractedly. "Look Mum's obviously not through there, is she? Or, is she? Come on Jen, think – you should know."

"Private Patients" says Jenny. "Chance would be the thing, wouldn't it, eh? Anyway, I don't think they have private psycho wards".

"Don't use that word" Emma hisses.

"What? PP?. Oh I know, look, we've missed it. It's back there, then left, down the stairs."

Emma glares at her sister's backview as Jenny strides towards the stairwell, where she points triumphantly at the floor guide.

Emma catches her up, grabs Jenny's arm forcing her to turn and look at her.

"What's the matter now? You've got a face like a slapped backside?"

"You'll have one if you don't shut up with your wise cracks. This isn't funny".

"Oh Em." Jenny reaches out towards her sister who shrugs her off and starts down the stairs.

"Em, Emma. I'm sorry. All right?" She has to raise her voice as Emma's head disappears temporarily out of sight. "Emma, wait" Jenny shouts.

Emma stops two flights down, and waits, her fingers drumming impatiently on the cold, clammy handrail

"Will you stop shouting"? she orders as Jenny reaches her. "Look this must be it – you did say Valency ward, didn't you?"

Their eyes travel to the sign now right in front of them. Psychiatric wards – Valency and Tamar.

Emma senses Jenny trembling, all bravado gone, as they enter Valency ward. Within everything is brightly coloured, yellow curtains emphasising the sunshine pouring in through the enormous windows. There seems to be, within this one ward, numerous doorways off a central area, where people are sitting, as if in a hotel lounge, some sipping coffee, looking at magazines, chatting. Most of the doors are ajar, or wide open to reveal not the expected metal bedded cell, but varying sizes of carpeted bedrooms with pretty bedding and fixtures. There are photographs on bedside tables and pictures on walls – almost homely.

CHAPTER THREE

The two women hesitate. There doesn't seem to be a reception desk of any kind, and not a uniform in sight. A smartly dressed woman who has been sitting chatting to two elderly women, on spotting Jenny and Emma, excuses herself and gets to her feet. She crosses the room her hand extended, and wearing a smile which lights up her whole face – a bright beacon in a sea of dreariness.

Jenny and Emma havn't moved from the door which they are both aware has closed and locked automatically behind them. They both start as they hear an eerie, heart rending wail. However, the woman is almost upon them her face reassuringly wreathed in smiles of welcome.

"You must be Anna's daughters – she was right - daughters to be proud of".

Jenny looks down at the floor, while Emma blushes for the two of them.

"Can we see our mother?" Jenny asks.

"Of course, of course. We wanted you to be here. So glad you've come. Look, follow me. She's in the office – this way".

The woman, (call me Abby), shows them into a a small, dull room with a couple of brown plastic chairs against one wall, and two more in the centre of the room.

Anna is sitting, looking very small in one of the centre chairs whist a suited doctor sits opposite her.

At the sight of her mother, Emma bursts into tears. The doctor gets hurriedly, or as hurriedly as a man of his bulk can, to his feet. He shakes Jenny and Emma heartily by the hand. Then he motions to the other chairs.

"I'm Dr Hart, and you must be Mrs du Bois' daughters." He looks from Emma to Jenny, and back again. "Please don't upset yourselves. Your mother is going to be fine – you'll see. Everything has just got a bit too much for her, that's all. It happens. Please do sit down" and Dr Hart plonks himself back down in his chair opposite Anna.

"Shit happens", mutters Jenny under her breath. Then, gesturing towards her mother. "That's all! Look at her."

Anna is looking away from the man who has been talking to her for what seems ages, not that she has been listening, not properly, not at all in fact since he first opened his mouth. She has been resting in her mind – quite easy to do in here, except for this suit whoever he was.

"Mum. Mum. You OK?" Jenny asks, trying to rein in her mothers' attention. Anna turns her head, and looks up, first at Jenny, and then at Emma, switching her gaze from one to the other for several seconds before she speaks.

"Oh girls, where's Lucy? Is she all right?"

"Lucy? Aunty Lucy?" Jenny shrugs her shoulders. "Well, I, we don't know really," she answers, glancing at Lucy and raising her eyebrows. "But if you want to see her, I'll try and phone her as soon as we get back. Havn't got her number with me. Do you want to see her then?"

Anna smiles suddenly, a small 'I can do this' sort of smile.

"Now then," The doctor leans towards Anna. "Can you tell me what the date is today?"

Anna's' smile fades, and she frowns back at the doctor.

"The date? Why, it's Thursday, isn't it? I've never been very good with dates."

"What about this one then? Who is the Prime Minister at the moment?"

Emma places a protective arm around Anna's shoulders, while Jenny stares hard at her mother, willing her to answer. She knows the answer, she must do, but Anna doesn't answer. She seems to have gone away from them all, slumped backwards now in her chair, her expression completely blank – closed down.

The doctor clears his throat, rubs his chin.

"I think what your mother needs right now is a nice long sleep – complete rest. She is totally exhausted."

Jenny turns on the doctor.

"Don't talk about Mum, as if she isn't here. Talk to her." She orders.

The doctor sighs. He has seen it all before, heard it all before, but he turns his full attention to Anna anyway.

"Anna, we'd like you to stay with us tonight – here in the hospital, like you did last night. That, you'll get a really good night's sleep, and we can talk again in the morning, when you are all nice and fresh."

No response from Anna. The doctor gives Jenny an 'I told you so' sort of look.

"I'll get someone to take your mother to her room." He gets to his feet and makes for the door, but Jenny is barring his way.

"We'll take her. Come on Mum." Both girls help Anna gently to her feet and steer her out of the poky little room, and into the main area where they wait to be told what to do by people they don't know.

Abby appears, seemingly from nowhere, and takes Anna's arm.

"Let's get you settled down in your nice warm bed. Your girls can come and see you when you're all tucked up. Come along."

"I can't believe that Mum is letting her talk to her like that, like she's a child, or gaga, or something." Jenny fumes as they watch their mother being led away.

Emma flinches at her sister's choice of words.

"She, Mum, is not gaga as you call it," she hisses uncharacteristically.

"No, I know. I didn't say she was. Oh Christ Em, what are we doing here, any of us?"

"Dunno, just don't know, but s'pose we had better just wait. You going to phone Aunt Luce, or am I?"

"Oh I don't know. See when we get back eh? God, I'm dying for a ciggie."

"So am I, and I don't smoke." Emma almost laughs. "Uh oh who's this?"

A red haired woman is approaching them. She introduces herself as the ward manager, Elaine

"You must be Anna's daughters, Jenny and Emma."

"How do you know our names?" Jenny asks. Elaine smiles.

"Your mother is certainly not very well at the moment, but she still knows your names. She told me, and very proud of you both she is too."

"She is talking then? That's a relief" Emma sighs. "She had us worried in there, didn't she Jen?"

"She will be OK. Try not to worry. If you'd like to pop in and say goodbye. I'll get someone to show you where she is. And don't be afraid to ring us – anytime"

Elaine turns away leaving Emma and Jenny staring blankly at one another. Emma speaks first.

"Is that it then? She's got to stay here?"

Jenny suddenly tugs Emma by the arm.

"Let's go back and ask God."

CHAPTER FOUR

Dr Hart is just getting to his feet, as Emma and Jenny burst in. They havn't knocked. He motions them to sit down. Both women sit, although Jenny is only just about perched on the edge of the plastic chair. Dr Hart settles back down again making himself comfortable like a chicken settling onto its' nest.

"How can I help"? he asks, kindly enough.

"Has our mother really got to stay here? In a locked ward"? Jenny starts, trying to keep her voice even, steady.

"Well, we think it would probably be best to keep your mother in for a few days, just to assess her – see if we can find out exactly what's happening. I might know more about what's going on after a couple more sessions with her, but it would be pretty unusual. These things take time to....."

"But it happened so suddenly," Jenny interrupts. "One day she's right as rain, and the next, she's in here."

"Hmmm, I suspect this has been coming on for quite a while, and that your mother hasn't been as right as rain, as you put it, for some time."

Jenny flinches inwardly.

"We see her as much as we can but we've got children, husbands, stuff going on, one of us should have noticed...

"I am sure it's nobody's fault. We don't always notice these things in our nearest and dearest."

"So she really has got to stay here then? Locked up?" Emma looks horrified.

"I know this must seem awful, but your mother is not seeing things the way you are. I really do believe that it is best for her to stay here, just for now. We'll just see how we go, shall we? Take it one day at a time. But, tell me, has your mother ever behaved like this before?"

"I wouldn't say so, no, not ever. Jen?"

"No. she always seems to be busy, and we thought she was happy enough. I know she still misses Dad, probably always will, but she's never mentioned feeling really depressed or anything."

"Sometimes, that can be the hardest thing for someone who is depressed to do. Tell anyone, especially their families, their children, possibly for fear of undermining them, frightening them.

"What sort of life would you say your mother has had to date? Happy? Miserable? What?"

Jenny and Emma look at one another. Jenny shrugs.

"Well, she's had the usual stresses, like everyone else" says Emma. "Her father left her mother when Mum was just a baby. It wasn't easy for Gran, or for Mum, growing up without a father."

"And she's had breast cancer," adds Jenny.

Dr Hart is making notes, strange little squiggles on his notepad that presumably he, and he alone, can decipher.

"I see, and how did she appear to deal with that?"

"Appear? She didn't appear to do anything. She dealt with it brilliantly actually." Jenny said defiantly. "Just had a mastectomy, and got on with it. Our parents ran a lavender farm in France. She said she didn't have time to be ill, but then Dad died, and more recently, our grandmother, so....."

Jenny trails off. She looks so sad, that Emma reaches across and squeezes her hand until she gets a weak smile in return.

"And, would you say you were close to your mother, both of you?"

"I'd say yes, definitely, wouldn't you Em?"

"Well we both see her a couple of times a week, if that's what you mean. She always seems fine, cheerful. Think we get on pretty well as families go."

"And you havn't noticed anything strange in her behaviour lately – anything you thought odd?"

"Odd? What do you mean, odd?" Jenny smiles to herself. "Well, she is Mum. Sorry, no that sounds awful. It's just that she's always been such a strong character – in the nicest possible way. I told her she was becoming eccentric a few weeks ago. She seemed to quite like the idea, laughed, called me cheeky, and said I was probably right."

Dr Hart looks up from his doodling and smiles encouragingly.

"And what brought that on? Why did you call her eccentric?"

"Oh, I don't know. She does funny things sometimes – you know, wearing strange things, things that don't go, and putting sugar in the fridge, milk in the sugar bowl – that sort of thing."

"I don't think she's really been the same since Gran died," Emma says sadly. "You don't think that that's what has brought all this on, this well, sort of breakdown, or whatever it is?"

Both women look expectantly at the doctor, but are disappointed.,

"Hard to say. Early days," is all he says as he lumbers to his feet. The interview seems to be over. Dropping his pen and notebook into his briefcase, he snaps it shut, and holds the door open saying "Abby will come back in a minute and show you where your mother is staying. Goodbye for now." He shakes them both heartily by the hand, and strides off leaving them waiting a good ten minutes for Abby to appear. When she does, she ushers them along to a pretty pink bedroom down a corridor off the main sitting room.

Anna is propped up in bed, and she is sleeping peacefully. The women hesitate, then creep away, no longer grown up daughters, adults, but children, and frightened.

As soon as they get outside the building, Jenny lights a cigarette, inhaling deeply. They have not spoken since they left their mother. Emma breaks the silence.

"This is surreal, Jen. What if nothing changes, and she never gets better? What if this is it? What if she's got to stay here for ever?"

Jenny is fumbling for her car keys at the bottom of her handbag, her cigarette clamped between her lips.

"God, I'm going to have to empty the whole bloody thing." She mutters, as she removes the cigarette, and draws in a deep breath. "Oh, got them. What are you staring at me like that for? She won't – have to stay here for ever, course she won't. It came, so it'll go, whatever it is. Look, I'm off now, well when I've finished this. Call me later, and don't forget, you promised to phone Aunt Luce. Ok?"

Emma doesn't remember promising anything, but it's not worth arguing about.

"Yeh. Ok. See you then" She gives Jenny a brief kiss on the cheek, and heads off to the car park. "Oh and love to the littlies," she calls back over her shoulder.

"And mine to the teenies, Jenny calls as she leans back heavily against the cold stone building. She finishes her cigarette, drops it, and grinds it underfoot before following Emma to the car park.

CHAPTER FIVE

"We're not going. What part of we're not going, don't you understand?"

"Oh, very flip. Yes, you're so good at being flippant, aren't you Nigel?"

"Look, if it's just standing there empty. I don't think Anna's ever going to come back and live there. In fact I know she isn't so why can't we......"

"No, but it must be very nice for her knowing she can." Nigel sneers. He has been furious ever since Lucy had turned up back at the flat telling him that the cottage was not theirs and they would have to move back to London.

"You never wanted to spend more than five minutes there when it was our supposed home. You were always here, presumably. Could have been anywhere for all I knew."

Nigel turns away to look out of the small paned window down into the wet windblown street below,

Lucy sits on the bed looking at his angry back. That's all she's seen of him for months she realizes, apart from his sulky face across the meal table.

"Maybe if you hadn't done such a stupidly obscure degree, we could have afforded to buy the place from her." Nigel turns towards her. "How can you be so thick?. Beats me how you ever got into university, never mind leaving with a first. Who did you have to sleep with?"

"How dare you? How could you Nigel, say that to me? Anyway, how am I thick? I'm the one with the job, career."

"And I thought women were supposed to be the sensitive ones" Nigel sneering again.. "You just don't get it do you?"

"Get what?" Lucy turns her palms up in a gesture of miscomprehension, or is it despair? "What's to get?"

"That it's not about money. I wouldn't set foot in that bloody cottage if she paid me, but it should have been left to you – it was our ticket out of here."

"And you say it's not about money. Why did you marry me Nigel – not for the family holiday home surely?"

"Because I thought we had a future, you and I. We grew up together for God's sake."

"Well, on and off."

"You know what I mean, those first years, then the holidays at the cottage".

"Look I left Sycamore Drive when I was five, and you only came to the cottage twice, from what I remember"

"I would have come more often if I'd been invited, but your precious father only ever invited Anna, bloody pervert. Anyway he never liked me. Actually told me once that I got on his nerves. Huh!"

"He was very fond of Anna"

"Obviously very fond." Nigel snorts.

Lucy ignores the innuendo, doesn't bite.

"I know he always felt sorry for Mary and Anna after Derek walked out. We always seemed to be involved with next door, and Anna and me, we were so close, when we were young, more like sisters really, and Anna did come down to the cottage a lot. Well, until…. well, at first." Lucy is frowning, forgetting Nigel for a few seconds, remembering something else confused by threads of memory."

"But later, going to the same Uni." Nigel is almost whining now. Why would he whine? "Must have been meant. We're good together, Luce."

"In bed maybe. But even that's worn a bit thin, wouldn't you say?"

"Only because you keep banging on about babies." Nigel spits the last word out

"You say babies as if they are a species of pet dog that I expect you to go up in a rocket and get me from another planet."

"Honestly Luce, you do talk a load of rubbish sometimes."

Lucy sits on the edge of the bed, tired now, really tired, and Nigel stands by the window, less than three feet away, wishing he lived someone else's life, anyone else's. He sighs, and turns back towards her, sitting on the bed looking small and vulnerable. His voice softens.

"We don't need a baby, Luce. We've got each other."

So why the affairs? she thinks, but looks up at him tiredly, tries to smile. She can't see his face, his back is to the light, but she knows from his tone that it has softened. The battle, this one, is over. Peace until the next. Is it going to be a long war, she wonders. She is tired of walking on eggshells. Tired as she is, of all of it, underneath she is angry, but as ever, is hiding it. She can't face another big row. Nigel would only storm out again, find someone else, yet another someone else.

"I'll go and fix us some supper shall I?"

"No, no, let's go out. Yes I know, we can't afford it, but hell. Look, don't change. We'll go as we are to the Italian. Lots of pasta and even more of the house red." Yes?

He's asking for forgiveness, trying, Lucy thinks.

"Well at least let me eput some make up on, and I've been in these horrible work clothes all day" She thought, but didn't say how much nicer it had been to work from home, back in Cornwall, no need to dress up in ghastly suits and heels, no rush hour. Now, back in London, she was expected to work at the office.

"Look if we're going to walk, why don't we have a glass of wine here first? And Nigel – you know you're probably right anyway. It might seem a bit weird, spending time there now – after everything that's happened. It's not home anymore, and our work is here. I do realize, you've proved it often enough – that you would rather be in London." Nigel lets the last part of Lucy's speech go, and crosses to the door but turns back. Last word Nigel.

"Don't you wonder though Luce? I mean why he didn't leave you the cottage. It makes no sense, seems so unfair. You're his only daughter. Anyway, I'll get you that glass of wine." He leaves the room, smiling one of his charming, but rare smiles.

Lucy sighs, relieved to have a minutes peace as she steps out of her skirt and places it neatly over the back of a chair.

She rummages in a drawer, and takes out her favourite sweater. It is old, but it was expensive, good quality, and she always feels comfortable in it, cosy. She slips into her jeans and sits down at the little dressing table and stares into her blue eyes.

Hello, she says in her head. How are you doing? Tough sometimes isn't it, forgiving, starting over? It is her mothers' voice and it comforts her. She hears it often, feels her mothers presence. She had been still at University when the accident happened. A drunk driver who survived to rot in jail, wiped Stella and Clive off the planet. Lucy had been coming home for the Easter vacation. She went still, not to a chocolate and daffodil celebration, but to arrange the double funeral.

Anna had come down, and between them they had sorted everything out. Lucy went to Paris, and stayed with Anna for the rest of the vacation. Then she went back to University, and Nigel. They decided that they would spend the summer at the cottage, and the Christmas holidays. With only a few months to go before graduation, they made their plans. Nigel proposed, and just before they graduated, they had married quietly and romantically in the University chapel. They couldn't afford to go abroad, but went straight down to the cottage. They would live in Cornwall in the cottage, have babies, Nige, had actually said that once. He would get a job, no problem. They would be happy.

Silly kids, that's what we were, and now we're even sillier grown-ups, Lucy thinks as she applies fresh lipstick and tries to smile at herself. Hard to smile when you're so tired. Still, mustn't mention being tired. Nigel would take it as a personal attack. "You coming? Your wine wants attention. Do you want it in there? You're not going to be much longer are you?"

"Coming." Lucy calls, trying to sound enthusiastic. She looks longingly at the bed as she crosses to the door.

CHAPTER SIX

Nigel is shouting up from the street. "Come on. What are you doing now?. We're going to be late. Pete and Judy will be there already." Lucy rushes out of the front door, banging it behind her. "The phone. Some sort of message from Emma. Thought I'd better get it."

"Emma? Emma who?"

Lucy looks at Nigel in disbelief. "Emma, stupid. You know, Emma and Jenny?"

"Huh! What do they want? Phoning to tell us this flat's not actually ours, but theirs?"

"Don't be so bloody facetious. No, something about Anna, not being well. It was all jumbled up – the message. I'll phone in the morning. Are we walking then?"

Nigel is waving his arms in the air, not listening.

"A taxi! That's a bit of luck. Let's treat ourselves – save time, hate being late for Pete – bangs on about it all evening, and it's going to rain anyway. Won't matter on the way back, we'll be so pissed. Here, come on."

Nigel opens the taxi door and they get in, just as the heavens open.

"Huh, stroke of luck that. What's this about Anna? Getting bored with her precious cottage, is she?"

"What's that got to do with anything? That's all water under the bridge. Anna's ill"

"Might be water under the bridge for you – the last straw for me"

"What do you mean by that?"

"Oh nothing, nothing. She always was a bit odd, though, wasn't she?"
"Who? Anna? Odd?"
"Well, you know. Quiet's probably a better word. Don't think she ever liked me very much. Always seemed a bit sort of closed up."

To you maybe, Lucy thought, but didn't say.
"Mmm. Not always. She was happy enough when we were young, and things weren't easy for her and Mary back then. No, Anna was always like a ray of sunshine." You knew her then, you must remember? We had a great time – till I had to move away."
"Seems like a lifetime away".
"Doesn't it just?"

CHAPTER SEVEN

Later, much later spoons in a drawer.
"I know we all think Anna is a bit odd, but it's not her fault. Nigel, Nigel, are you awake?" Lucy sits up disentangling herself from the vine of Nigel's body.

"I am now. What are you on about?"

"It's serious isn't it, this? It's not as if she's having a breakdown and next week she's going to be all better – you know back to normal"

Nigel snorts.

"Hey you" Lucy reaches across him and flicks his bedside light on.

"Hey yourself." Nigel, irritably. "Turn your own light on"

"Well you're being cruel. Poor Anna lying in that dreadful place away from her pets and her home."

"Her home! Our home, that was! Huh! Anyway, there's nothing we can do about anything at this time of night whatever time it is" He squints at the clock on the bedside table "Ten to bloody three.! For God's sake, go to sleep."

Nigel turns over, switches off the light, and cuddles himself back to sleep.

Lucy lies blinking into the darkness. A cup of tea? She asks herself. Would have been nice if Nigel had offered. Huh, fat chance. He was right though, there was nothing she could do at this time of night. Probably nothing she could do anyway, and that was the worst thought of all, and one which sends her off into a fitful thickly dreamed sleep until she is briefly but not rudely woken to the sound of the birds. Those bloody birds as Nigel called them on a daily basis, but which Lucy quite liked – dawn chorus and all that.

Dozing off again, this time into a deep and peaceful sleep, she was awoken not by the birds, nor as she might have wished, Nigel bringing her tea in bed. He might if she stays there long enough, but she never could wait once she was properly awake. Lucy turns and looks at the empty side of the bed. He must be downstairs making some tea. She closes her eyes again. She can hear something – just, but it's not birdsong. The birds must have all gone out for the day, hunting and gathering, or whatever it was they did.

It was the phone – the bloody phone. Why doesn't he answer it? Angry now, Lucy stomps out of bed, grabbing her dressing gown from the end of the bed and pads downstairs in her bare feet. The phone in the kitchen is trilling for England.

"Nigel, where are you? The phone." She picks it up, whilst at the same time hearing the boiler cutting in. Bloody man is in the shower.

"Hello, yes," she says, pushing the haystack that is her hair, out of her eyes. It slips straight back across her face, as always.

"Emma? O yes, I know, I was supposed to phone you. Sorry..... What?..... Meet at the hospital you mean?...... O.K...... Oh straight there...... No, we'll put up somewhere".

She doesn't register Emma's sigh of relief. "Yes see you then. Oh, hang on, how is she, Anna?..... Oh, no s'pose it is. O.K. see you later."

CHAPTER EIGHT

"Christ, look at this rain" Nigel hesitates, his hand on the door handle. "I'm not getting out in this."

"Let's wait a bit. Anyway I can't see Jenny or Em's cars anywhere".

"How could you?" Nigel snaps irritably "There's over a hundred cars here, and anyway you can't see anything for this sodding rain."

"Don't snap at me. It's not my fault it's raining."

Lucy looks at Nigel's profile and at the muscle twitching in his cheek – always a bad sign that. What did he have to be so irritable about anyway? Sometimes she really thought she hated him.

They sit in silence, but for the swishing of cars coming and going, voices carried on the rainy gusts, umbrellas blown inside out – curses. They wait; half the car full of fury.

"I wonder if she knows we're coming, if they've told her" Lucy ventures, more for something to say than anything else. Of course they would have told her – whoever they were. Anna couldn't have turned into a gibbering idiot overnight, beyond comprehension.

"I expect she knows. Soon everyone will know."

"What on earth do you mean by that? Know what precisely? What's the matter with you? Nigel?"

Nigel sighs a long sigh as if he has been holding his breath for ever. He relaxes his grip on the steering wheel, takes a deep breath and turns towards her, his face softening, "I'm sorry Luce. I'm just being me – bad tempered, grouchy old me, and you're right, none of this is your fault. How could it be?"

He leans towards her and strokes her face pushing the hair back gently holding it there off her face.

"I do love you. You do know that, don't you?"

"Well, you keep coming back. Got to be something keeping us together, I suppose, but I can't think what." She gives a wry smile.

Nigel lets his hand drop and turns in his seat to look, instead of at her, at the still pouring rain.

"Now you're talking about children again I suppose – bit late for all that isn't it, surely? I mean, your biological clock must have been well and truly overwound if it's still ticking on. We're just too old now. For God's sake face it."

"Nigel Don't be so mean. You don't realize, things you say sometimes. I was just being flippant, you know, trying to lighten the mood, and you have to jump in with all that....."

"Rain's stopping. Nigel interrupts her. "I'm sorry old girl, just call me Jekyll or was it Hyde – you know, the nasty one."

Old girl, old, too old. Lucy nibbles bitterly at the words as she gets out of the car glad to be in the rain freshened air, dreading going into the depths of the hospital. Nigel locks the car, comes round and slips an arm about her shoulder.

"Come on then, let's go and visit the mentally challenged."

"Oh no, the pervert's with her."

"Shh Jen, they'll hear you. Aunt Lucy, Hi. We've been told to wait here. Come and sit down." Emma crosses the corridor and kisses her Aunt on the cheek, then ushers her to sit next to Jenny who is almost scowling at Nigel – Uncle Nigel.

"Well hello girls. How are you both? Looking as bonny as ever"

"Oh Nigel, for heavens sakes, they stopped being bonny years ago, though that's not to say they aren't both absolutely gorgeous."

"Oh hear, hear. Sorry girls."

He winks at a stony faced Jenny.

Thick skinned sod. Why doesn't he drop dead? Do us all a favour, Jenny thinks almost out loud, almost so that he can hear the trace of her words.

CHAPTER NINE

"Well, well, well." Lucy tries to sound light as she enters Anna's room, but there is a catch in her voice. "What the hell are you doing in here?"

She crosses to the bed.

"The nurse," she nods over her shoulder. "The nurse says you won't get up today. Anna?"

Anna is propped up in bed. She gives Lucy a brief, resigned glance with no sign of recognition.

Christ! Lucy feels a jolt beneath her ribcage. She doesn't know me. She thinks I'm a nurse or something – a part of this place.

Anna has lost what flicker of interest she had in her visitor, and has turned her head away. Lucy pulls up a chair and sits close to Anna's bedside. She gently takes one of Anna's hands in her own, but Anna pulls it away without even looking at her.

"Anna, Anna, it's me – Lucy. Yes?"

No response. Nothing. Anna doesn't even turn her head. She seems engrossed in the treetops outside the window, concentrating on them, almost as if she is counting the branches. Her fingers clutch the cover tightly about her.

"Oh Anna, I hate to see you like this. I'm sorry I didn't keep in touch. I wasn't sulking, not really. It was just that I was so hurt, so upset, and I think Nigel's going to leave me. He's being really quite nice at the moment, welt most of the time. Even says he loves me, but I think he's found someone else, someone different to all the others, someone he's really going to leave me for. Anna, are you listening?"

Anna makes no sound or movement, and Lucy bursts into tears. She gazes at Anna through blurry eyes, but there isn't a flicker of a response –nothing. Lucy pulls a tissue out of her handbag and blows her nose loudly.

"Excuse me", she sniffs, then smiles lightly to herself. She gets to her feet, gathers up her coat and bag. She places a carrier bag on the bed.

"I brought you a few things – you know, that smelly talc you always liked, things like that. Anna?"

Lucy presses the tissue hard against her nose, and waits, watching Anna, waiting for a response. Then she leaves the little bedroom, shutting the door quietly behind her.

A nurse smiles at her as they pass in the corridor. Lucy goes to speak, but changes her mind. Better get going. Nigel is waiting, and the girls will want to know how it went.

How it went indeed. What did they expect? What did she expect?. She doesn't know the answer, not really, feels shaken to the core, as if she has just suffered a great shock.

Anna isn't there for her any more – not there, if Lucy needs her, and she does need her, more than ever, but Anna has gone away. Lucy has no-one now. Nigel? He doesn't count – she knows that. Not any more.

CHAPTER TEN

Anna, Mrs Du Bois to you and me, is keeping her eyes tightly shut. She is so tired. Go away, go away. I love you, but please go. Take me back please – so that I can put things right, start again. Rewind. But you won't will you? No-one can, least of all me.

Silence. Peace. Peace, of a kind, but nothing's changed. I will never be free of it – not this. Tired – so very tired.

Hello yourself. Would I like something to help me sleep – wouldn't I? Something that will make me sleep until it's all over.

Then the white vision, the nurse, is gone. Everyone is finally gone. Anna opens one eye, just a fraction. Yes, everyone gone. Thank God. She turns her head to look out of the window and beyond into the whiteness. The window is filled with whiteness, no blue, no shades of grey – no spriggy treetops. Anna shudders, snuggles down as far as she can under the bedclothes, but keeping her eyes fixed on the window. A world of pure white. She is alone at last in a world of white – like that other time so very long ago. Had it really been her, in her lifetime?

She has wandered off towards the forest only a few yards from where the garden opened out onto the moorland. She wasn't afraid was she? She knows the forest well. The snow is deep, and Anna, just a four foot nothing twelve year old. The snow comes up to her knees, deep and crisp and .....How does it go? She closes her eyes, in the stillness, then she is wading deeper over the moorland and into the forest, the track or what she knows is the track, stretching before her, unmarked, pristine utterly beautiful. She scoops up a handful of snow, and puts it to her lips. It tastes of nothing. No, no, it tastes of snow. She can taste it even now. How she misses it. It never snows here, not now, not properly.

The sky was the brightest blue on that day, when she was twelve. She longs to go back there, to stay in that world of purity, of brightness, so far removed from the world of grey, or worse, of her other days.

Trouble comes though, even into a sleep of innocence of thought, of snow, and peace and purity. Setting the scene – innocent enough surely, but remembering threads of what is, what should but cannot be, completely forgotton. A reminder from whom? What? The past? The future?

The white world evolves. Whitewashed, but grubby walls in an open-ended garage.

CHAPTER ELEVEN

"He left, just left, and that's all I can tell you Darling. I'm sorry."

"What? Just like that? Something must have happened. Was it anything to do with me? Was it because of me?"

"Don't be ridiculous," Mary answers sharply. Too sharply and too quickly. She has been caught off guard, and she has never been very good at thinking on her feet. "How could it possibly have had anything to do with you? You were less than a day old"

Anna chews her bottom lip, studying her mother's face, her eyes. This conversation will come back to haunt her – another thread of memory.

"Didn't he want children then, my father?" she says at last. "Was that it?" she adds hopefully, as if a more positive answer, any more positive answer would do. She had always known that her father had walked out on them, but until now, has never pursued the matter, never felt the need – until now.

Mary sighs. This is ghastly. She feels sick, needs some air. What if Anna can tell that she is lying, lying to the most precious person in the world to her. She should have got her story straight, or a story, anyway for just this moment. She does know, understand that it is Clive's death that has set all this off. Bloody man, and poor, unlucky Stella. Probably driving too fast knowing Clive.

Since that terrible night, Lucy and Anna had been in constant touch, on the phone, leaving messages, texting. Anna had gone down straightaway, stayed for a few hours, come home, and then a few days later, gone back down for the funeral. She had to support Lucy. They were as close as sisters, but Lucy had Nigel to support her. To Mary though, Nigel was just a boy who had grown up on Sycamore Drive, gone to the same school as the girls, then even on to the same university. Well, the same one as Lucy anyway.

By this time apparently Nigel and Lucy were talking of marriage, but still Mary couldn't see Nigel as anything but a rather untidy little boy, with a thick shock of dark hair which always seemed to flop over one eye, making him look even more untidy. If Mary had been able to bring herself to go to the funeral, she would have met the grown-up Nigel. Anyway, what did all that matter now? No-one appeared to wonder or care why she hadn't gone. Why would they?

Anna had gone, of course, had accepted her mother's lame and unnecessary excuse without question and that had been that – end of an era. But now the ripples of repercussion.

CHAPTER TWELVE

The afternoon's discussion starts lightly enough. They have been for a long walk, and are more than ready for a sit down, and a cup of tea. Anna has been very quiet since she got back from the funeral, sort of withdrawn, preoccupied. As they stand in the kitchen waiting for the kettle to boil, Mary asks Anna what her plans are, now that she appears to have dropped out of university. She had arrived home pale, thin and depressed in the middle of the Spring term saying that the course wasn't for her. Mary hadn't gone into it or on about it, but had just let Anna be, looking after her as she always had done. Gradually Anna put on a bit of weight, and was beginning to look more like her old self, and then the bombshell from Lucy in a hysterical phone call in the middle of the night.

They have prepared the tea, and the sun has just started to pour in through the sitting room windows. Anna carries the tray through, and as she sets it down, the questions start, and Mary caught off guard is at a loss to respond to Anna's quick-fire interrogation.

Deep down, Mary knows that nothing short of the truth will do, but now? Now, this moment isn't the time, surely?..Anna is still only twenty. It would hurt her, shock her, Mary knows that, wants somehow to protect her daughter from the truth. She knows too that sequentially, she would be hurt too, maybe irrepairably. She offers up a silent prayer. Not now God, please not today.

"What's brought all this on?" she asks brightly, as she busies herself with the business of pouring the tea. She is playing for time, and she knows it. "Is it because of what happened – to Clive and Stella?"

Anna is sitting on the edge of her chair watching her mother pour the tea, count the sugar lumps, and push the plate of biscuits towards her.

"Er, no thanks Mum." Anna takes her cup of tea from Mary, and sits back balancing it awkwardly on her lap. "I suppose it is, in a way. Makes you think about things, life, stuff –you know. "Well, it's made me think, anyway, you know, about my father, how I'd feel, you know, if he died, just didn't exist anywhere, anymore. I know it's different for me, not like Lucy, but all the same. I guess it's just the not knowing."

Mary has sat down opposite Anna. She has left her cup and saucer on the tray, aware that she is trembling slightly. She takes a deep breath, and nudges herself to think for a couple of seconds before she speaks.

"Well, Darling, all I really know for certain, is that after he left, your father went to France, and, as far as I know, never came back. He wrote to me to say that we should keep the house until you got married, and then," Mary takes another deep breath. "Then, it was to be made over to you."

"Wow! Really? So he did love me a bit then?" Anna leans forward to study her mother's face. "Well, he wouldn't do that otherwise, would he?" Then again, maybe he would. Maybe he just felt guilty, abandoning us both like that. How come you've never mentioned this before Mum?"

"We thought it would be a nice surprise for you, you know when the time came, and of course for whoever you marry." lies Mary. She can, and she will give her precious and only daughter this, this gift of worth, the gift of believing she is loved. Well that bit, about being loved, that isn't a lie. Mary loves Anna enough for two doting parents.

"Is he still alive, do you think. Would anyone let us know if anything, anything awful had happened to him?"

"You would think so, wouldn't you? Yes, I'm sure someone would." Mary tries to sound reassuring. She leans over and pats Anna's hand. "It's a small world, after all."

What more can she say? What if Anna starts searching for Derek, and...Oh God, what if she finds him? It can be a very small world. Hasn't she just acknowledged that?

"Top up love?" Mary picks up the teapot, willing her hands not to shake, and determinedly tops up Anna's cup. She's hardly touched her own. "Please eat a biscuit, Darling" she urges.

Anna smiles, looking more relaxed than she has for weeks.

Much to Mary's relief, Anna doesn't mention her father again, but she seems to spend even more time than usual on the phone, or her mobile. If she isn't talking to Lucy, she is talking to Jenny in Paris. She seems so set on the idea of France that Mary knows she has to accept the situation, and hope for the best.

It isn't long before she is driving an excited Anna to the station. Mary waves her off as cheerily as she can manage, and drives tearfully and drearily back to her empty nest.

CHAPTER THIRTEEN

Much to Mary's surprise and joy, Anna calls from De Gaulle airport soon after she lands, and is even more touched when Anna phones every day for almost a week. Must be homesick, Mary tells herself, and it doesn't last, of course it doesn't. Anna, with Jenny's help has found a job almost within hours of arriving in Paris, has settled into Jenny's flat and everything appears to be running like clockwork.

On the Friday following Anna's departure on the Sunday, Mary hovers by the telephone. Well, she can't expect the poor girl to call home every day. She is twenty, for Heaven's sakes, but then the weekend slips by. She is probably out and about, seeing the sights, window shopping or whatever young women in Paris do at the week-end, especially their first week-end there. Still she hears nothing on Monday. Fair enough, Mary thinks, new country, new job. Anna is probably quite overwhelmed by it all.

When at the end of a very long, and dismal week however, and Mary has heard nothing, she decides that perhaps it's her turn to call her daughter. Why not?

"Hi Mum....,.Yes, fantastic......The job? Oh yes, brilliant, and the flat, and the people, yes, all good. And Lucy's here, Mum....Yes, arrived on Tuesday........Bit of a squeeze, yes, but poor thing, she's so down.... Well, apart from that, yes, and Jenny makes her laugh.....Yes, she always was, wasn't she? Are you Ok Mum? Sure?..Bet it's lovely and peaceful there". Mary looks around the silent hallway. "not like this madhouse. Oh believe me Mum, you wouldn't. It's chaos. Lucy? Well hard to say, really....certainly a week or two, 'till she feels better, able to face the cottage, you know, sorting everything out....No, not very nice......Nigel? Oh yes, he rings her every day...Well, rather her than me is all I'll say, but she needs someone, I suppose. I'll keep you posted...of course I will.....I expect they will.....Don't know yet. You'll know when the invite pops through the letter box! Anyway, gotta go, otherwise I'll miss my turn in the salle de bain again....Yes, hot date...Not really, but very nice, a tall dark handsome Frenchman. Yes, he works in an office, hates it, records or something. Got to go. Loads of love. Byee"

Mary puts the phone down. No mention of Derek. That was a relief, a bonus. Perhaps in all the excitement, Anna has forgotton her original purpose in going to France. Perhaps it wasn't that important to her after all. This whole new life that Anna is carving out for herself, one which separates mother and daughter, possibly for ever, is possibly more than enough to stop Anna looking backwards, even with a grieving Lucy staying with her.

Mary goes back into the sitting room and pours herself a glass of wine, the second this evening. She doesn't switch the television on, but sits in the glow of one small lamp, and stares into the fire.

For the first time since she heard the terrible news of the car crash, Mary thinks about Clive, not Derek, never Derek. In the early days of what seemed to be a potentially happy marriage, Clive and Stella moved into Sycamore Drive, next door in fact. Clive had mesmerized Mary the first time she saw him. She didn't stand a chance. It had been easier, much easier when he and Stella and Lucy moved away, down to their cottage in Cornwall, but now Clive didn't even exist, not anywhere. She's not sure how she feels. And Stella-poor long suffering Stella. A brick, Clive had called her. She and Mary had never got on – it was as if they knew straightaway, on that first welcome to the neighbourhood drink that they could never be friends, and they hadn't. An antagonism, a tacit understanding of things not expressed, but known, what Clive laughingly called the cold war, existed between the two women.

Eventually, apart from the brief telephone arrangements about Anna's trips down to Cornwall, to visit Lucy, the two women never spoke. Clive always made the arrangements.

CHAPTER FOURTEEN

"Daddy, why doesn't Anna's mummy like me?"
"What? What are you babbling about now?"
"I like playing with Anna. She's my best friend. She's nice, but I don't like her Mummy"

"Don't be silly, course you do. You're round there all the time, or she's round here."

"But her mummy never comes round here. I don't think she likes Mummy, and everybody likes Mummy. And Daddy, where's Anna's daddy? I've never even seen him, have you? Is he a friend of yours?"

Stella walks in from the kitchen.

"Supper in about ten minutes, you two. Whatever's the matter Clive? You look as though you've seen a ghost" Stella looks hard at her husband. Then, thinking she understands, nods at him.

"You've just got time to, you know, if you're quick," she says.

"I can't just pop in for ten minutes. Honestly, this is getting ridiculous"

Clive gets slowly to his feet, his shoulders tensed. "I don't think I can take much more of this" He crosses to the window. Mothers and children walking up the avenue from school.. One woman, seeing him at the window, stops, kneels down to tuck in her small son's shirt, and push the flop of hair out of his eyes. She catches Clive's eye, and holds his gaze. Then she moves on to the end of the street where she has been living for the past seven years. Clive watches her. She hasn't kept well. Thank God he didn't, or rather thankyou Dad, that he didn't. He had expected Andrew to nudge him to the registry office, a shotgun in his back. But Andrew knew a good sort when he saw one. He liked strong, capable women. Besides Stella was what he called a looker He admired beautiful women.

"You don't have to marry the girl – not these days. Just get on with your nuptials old son. That girl of yours – she's the one for you, not that mousy little thing" was Andrews' advice to his son. The subject was never broached again.

Clive realizes that Stella is speaking. He shakes himself, turns from the window, his expression unfathomable – too much. Stella, her eyebrows raised in indignation is saying

"I said what do you mean? You can't take much more of this?

It was you who wanted it this way. We've, I've just gone along with you for the sake of the you know whos."

"What's 'diculous Daddy? Who's you know whos? I know it's somebody 'cos you and who is somebody, isn't it?"

Stella and Clive look down at their daughter as she lies on the floor with crayons and a colouring book. She has a crayon gripped between her teeth, and her brow is furrowed as if she is trying to work something out.

"Take that out of your....." Stella and Clive in unison. The little girl looks up from one to the other.

"I know, take that out of your mouth, you'll swallow it – you always say that, but I never do. Can I see Anna before bed?"

"No", again in unison.

"You put those colouring things away now, and go up for your bath young lady, and Clive, you'd better – well you know, if you're going to. I'll hold supper back."

"I'm listening" Lucy crows as she gets up from the floor. "You gotta secret. What is it? Tell me, tell me."

Clive looks tenderly at his daughter, and sighs. He sits heavily back down in the armchair.

"Yes, we have, and I think it's time we told you, don't you Stella?"

Stella, who is about to go back to the kitchen, stops in her tracks, looking back at Clive with a mixture of astonishment and horror.

She has gone as white as a sheet, and is holding tightly to the door handle. She is not thinking of Mary, nor even of her precious Lucy. She remembers – doesn't want to. Was it only yesterday? That woman, the one on the corner. Yes, turning into the avenue, Clive driving. The woman, Jo was it? Standing in the garden shears in hand.

She had asked Clive why she was staring at them, at him.

"Must be my devilish charm" Clive had answered. "and would you have me any other way?"

"She never speaks though – not to me. Even if I bumped right into her, I don't think she would"

"Don't you worry your pretty head. She's a bit young for you anyway. What could you have in common?" Clive pats Stella's knee, leaves his hand there. She glances at his profile. She thinks, but doesn't say – thanks for that. You really don't know you're doing it, do you; or do you?

"She lives with her parents, doesn't she?"

"She's still young, yes, but not that young. Can't be much fun stuck out in the suburbs with aged parents, and apparently, no husband."

"Either a saint or more likely, a sinner." Clive chuckles as they turn into the cul de sac. He uncharacteristically crashes the gears swearing viley, and so much in character. Stella says nothing. She's a good sort. She knows it's Mary she should be thinking of, but it had been her own fault – Mary's. She could have said no, from the word go.

Clive clasped his hands between his knees, takes a deep breath.

"I'll go round after supper, Stell, and I'll tell them what I'm about to tell you. Why don't you sit down for a minute?"

"Clive. Is this a good idea?". She sits teetering on an arm of the sofa. "And tell me what?"

"You know, what we were talking about the other day. You know, the cottage – what a waste it is, owning that and renting this. Well, why don't we just up sticks, decamp, and start again in Cornwall – a fresh start."

"Cornwall!" Stella and Lucy in unison this time. What? Really go and live there. But what about.....?

"Can Anna come too, and her mummy? I know she's not very nice, but it might make her happy, then she'd be nicer."

Clive is shaking his head in disbelief.

"Never mind the neighbours. You'll be wanting that ragamuffin, what's his name again? Nigel isn't it to come and live with us next?"

"Are we really going to live in Cornwall, Daddy?"

"It's up to your mother. What do you think Stell? Would be a lot healthier all round if you ask me. Otherwise, I'm afraid little Agatha Christie here......"

CHAPTER FIFTEEN

Lucy is helping Anna to pack in the beamed bedroom which runs the length of the cottage.

"Good midnight feast, wasn't it Anna? I said....."

Anna stops in the middle of stuffing a sweater into her bag, and turns on Lucy.

"You can be so childish sometimes Luce. Midnight feast! Is that really all you've got to think about?"

Lucy flushes, stops what she is doing, looks down. "No" says the ugly, smokey, grey cloud. "It isn't all she has to think about, and you should know better."

"Will you still be coming for Christmas" She asks, feeling the negativity in the room, emanating from Anna, and knowing the answer, or the gist of it anyway. Anna doesn't hesitate, knows she doesn't need to think anything up – Lucy would believe, accept anything she told her.

"No, Mum needs me. She can't spend every Christmas on her own just because he wants to play Father Christmas.

"You always liked coming down here though, didn't you?"

"Yes, of course, but Mum never likes it when I come. Always makes me, and then she acts as if everything is my fault – as if I've deserted her, wanted to, or something. I don't know. Anyway," more cheerfully, "it's Jenny's birthday on Saturday. You remember Jenny; my best friend. Anyway she's having a party."

The girls fall silent. Anna goes on packing, stuffing things into her holdall, her back turned to Lucy while Lucy stares at Anna's back, biting

45

her bottom lip. They both want to cry, to cling to each other, but they don't, won't, not ever,

"Come on you two" Stella calls up the stairs. "Anna, Clive will take you to the train. I've got to stay here. The egg man's coming – got to pay him."

"You coming? Anna asks over her shoulder as she drags her bag off the bed, and heads for the stairs. Lucy follows her silently as Anna bump, bump, bumps her bag all the way down to the landing. Lucy glances idly at the little window over the garage, then stops, peers through it.

"Think I'll stay here." She says heavily. "With Mum."

They all stand about in the drive. Clive chucks Anna's holdall into the boot.

"Come on then. Am I escorting both of you lovely young ladies today?"

Lucy looks away.

"You not going Lucy?" Stella asks. "Lucy?"

Lucy turns away from the scene. She can't stand it.

"No", she says defiantly, and runs off into the shrubbery.

Stella is hugging Anna, kissing her on both cheeks, saying goodbye. Clive watches them as he slams the boot lid down, and Lucy, hiding behind the lilac tree watches him watching.

"Not much of a goodbye was it? I thought you girls were bosom pals," Clive says glancing at his watch. "Still, can't wait for miss sulky drawers, better get off, miss the train otherwise. Hop in lass."

Anna waves through the rear windscreen ostensibly at Stella, but deep in her heart at Lucy.

CHAPTER SIXTEEN

"It's great to see you Luce, don't think we've even spoken since, well, you know."

Anna forces herself to say the words – still finds it difficult, as if it can't be true, as if she is making it up "Not since Phillippe's funeral."

Anna is meeting Lucy off the cross channel ferry.

"Well, apart from yesterday," Lucy laughs, takes Annas' arm and gives it an affectionate squeeze.

"Of course, apart from yesterday. Car's over here. Give me that, and I'll bung it in the boot."

The women cross the tarmac, Anna tanned and fit, next to an almost scrawny, pale Lucy. The tarmac is hot after a long summer day – steaming. They climb into the car, opening all the windows immediately, holding their breath to avoid sucking in the dry, suffocating heat..

"Blimey, it's hot, and I thought we were having a good Summer," says Lucy smiling at Anna who is turning the key and doing her seat belt up at the same time. "It's so good to see you Anna. Hope it's not inconvenient."

"Course not. A bit of a surprise, but a lovely one. Right, Le Lavande, here we come." And they swing out of the car park and up onto the big main road, but not for long. Soon, they are bowling along, down one pretty lane after another.

"Oh I do love France" Lucy sighs wistfully as the cornfields and the sleepy little villages slip past them. Then, "Not too much of a surprise, I hope?" she prompts.

Anna says nothing. She is concentrating on negotiating the twisty lane ahead.

"What? No, told you – lovely." Anna glances sideways at Lucy, readies across and pats her arm. "Really!"

"It's just that, well, why I came, sort of suddenly like this. I had this brainwave. Least I thought it was a brainwave – more of an idea really, probably daft. I was wondering, wondered"…….Lucy trails off.

"You surely havn't come all this way just because you wondered something? What is this brainwave of yours?" Anna asks, curiousity getting the better of her…

"Well, what I was thinking, wondering…" Lucy looks sideways at Anna. She feels suddenly shy, shy and silly. "Well, with Phillippe gone – sorry, probably not the best way of putting that, but I wondered if now, you might be thinking of coming home – you know, back to England. I told you on the phone, didn't I, Nigel's never home these days, always away – says it's business, and I expect some of it is, but…."

"You think he's messing about again?"

"Nigel? Of course he is, always has, always will, but I pretend not to notice – better that way. We get on well enough when he is home."

"In London, you mean?"

"Well no. He stays there a lot of the time, but I never leave Cornwall these days. First time I've set foot out of the county since, well you know – Phillippe.." Lucy glances sideways at Anna again to see if she has upset her, but Anna doesn't seem to be listening now, but concentrating on avoiding half a dozen scraggy chickens having a dustbath at the edge of the lane.

They turn sharply up a hill, the little car straining to get them to the top. They can't hear themselves speak anyway until they reach the top of the track, where they come to a sudden stop right in front of the farmhouse.

"Right, here we are. Can't wait to get out of this sticky little oven". Anna says with a sigh of relief, as she swings her legs out of the car, stands up and stretches. She stops to shove her head through the open window. "Why don't you go and freshen up, get settled in. Same room as usual. I'll meet you down on the terrace about six – with a lovely bottle of wine. I just need to go and ring the girls before they go out".

"Oh, give them my love". Lucy calls weakly as Anna rushes off into the cool of the house. "I'll get my stuff in" she adds to herself. She is tired, expected more of a welcome somehow. How did Anna always manage to make her feel like this? She had come all this way, and Anna hadn't really asked her why, not properly, as if she cared, and it was all for Anna after all, well, mostly. Silly the two of them on their own all the time.

CHAPTER SEVENTEEN

"Ah, there you are," Anna calls as Lucy, showered and refreshed, comes down the few steps to the terrace, stopping at the bottom to gaze across the fields of lavender, the vineyards and the distant Pyrenees, shimmering in the heat. The landscape is dotted with churches.

"Wow! Anna, this is so lovely. Can you, could you stay on here managing the lavender farm, harvesting and all that if you wanted to?"

Anna looks up sharply. She is in the middle of pouring out two glasses of ruby red wine.

"What do you mean – if I wanted to?" She hands a glass to Lucy. Her hand is trembling very slightly. Lucy doesn't appear to notice. "Why would I want to leave? I'm managing perfectly well – I have lots of help. Phillippe and I were so happy here, and after all we put into the place, and the girls, they love it – it's their home after all."

"Oh yes of course. I know, but they're both settled in England now, husbands, jobs, children, all that"

"Even so, it's still their home, where they grew up. They love coming back." Anna sips at her wine, her thoughts spoiling her appreciation. She pushes a dish of fat black olives towards Lucy.

Lucy straightens herself up in her chair, deciding to take the plunge. She'll never know if she doesn't ask.

"Well, I've come all this way, so I may as well tell you, or rather ask you. It's just – well – that as Nigel is away practically all the time. Things not too good on that front, as I told you in the car. What's new?

Yes, I know. Don't say it" Lucy throws her hands in the air in a gesture of despair which she can't negate with a laugh or a smile. "I just thought that perhaps you'd like to come home, you know, sell up here, and come back to England. You could come and share the cottage with me. It seems so big and empty, just me there rattling around on my own, and you know how you used to love it."

"Yes, I did, didn't I?" Anna looks away towards the mountains, her forehead furrowed. "I was a lot younger then though. Things change."

"Well yes, of course they do". Lucy is talking very quickly now. Was this such a good idea? "You've got the grandchildren now. Wouldn't you like to be able to see more of them, watch them growing up? Isn't that reason enough to come home? Think of it as retirement – couldn't you?"

Anna knocks back the remaining contents of her glass and quickly refills the two in silence.

"It's not too late, not these days. Not if you really wanted them."

"No but you do need, or anyway, I would, a willing partner, or some sort of support. Anyway, If I am honest, it probably is too late. I mean, can you just see me standing at the school gates with all those child-mums?"

Anna tuts and sighs. Poor Lucy. Not her fault, none of it. She'd been dealt a rotten hand, all right. Bloody Nigel –and bloody Clive.

Anna gets to her feet and smiles down at Lucy.

"Look, why don't I show you round the garden, then we can eat. Be nice to eat outside, wouldn't it? I got some lovely fresh sardines today at the market."

So the two women, glasses in hand, wander around the garden discussing plants, the weather, and chatting about the girls.

The next morning, they eat breakfast outside. Neither of them has slept well, especially Anna. They linger over their coffee until they are disturbed by a loud hooting sounding up the track. Anna starts. She has been jumpy all morning. Lucy has noticed but hasn't commented.

Now though, Lucy is utterly amazed to see unmistakeably the heads of Jenny and Emma as they alight from a small French hire car.

Anna avoids catching Lucy's eye, but flushes as she runs quickly up the steps to greet her daughters. She seems flustered, but not in the least surprised.

"Oh girls, you didn't need to rush out. I can deal with this. I just need to find the right moment."

Both young women hug their mother, then taking an arm apiece, they escort her across the yard, and around the corner of the house to where Lucy is waiting open-mouthed.

"Well", she says "I'm sure you havn't come all this way just to see me. You can always pop down to Cornwall to do that. If I'd only known, we could have travelled out together. So, tell me, do you often come home at the drop of a hat?"

Lucy waits for Jenny and Emma to come around the table to greet her. A kiss on the cheek wasn't too much to expect, was it?

CHAPTER EIGHTEEN

"Aunty Luce" they say in unison. Hardly a greeting really. Lucy feels hurt. The young women sit down. Jenny takes a swipe at a fly which has landed on her leg and bitten her.

"Bloody thing –only been here five minutes," she snaps irritably.

"Had any breakfast, you two?" Anna falls into nurturing mode.

"Yes, stuff on the ferry", Jenny says, but we'd both love some coffee, wouldn't we Em?

Look Mum, you sit down I'll make it. A big pot, then we can talk."

"Talk! That sounds all very serious." Lucy turns to Emma her eyebrows raised, but Emma just smiles briefly, and looks at her mother. The ensuing silence is unmistakeably awkward, and stretches on until Jenny comes back with the coffee on a tray. Lucy is beginning to feel distinctly outnumbered, unloved, but then she is used to feeling unloved.

"Hmm, that smells good, even though I have not long had coffee this morning." Says Anna brightly as she lifts the coffee pot and starts to pour. "Always smells, and tastes better when someone else makes it."

Silence as the four women sip, and gaze at the view, occasionally casting sideways looks at one another. They chat sporadically, about Phillippe, the lavender crop, lots of things.

They have now been sitting round the table for almost an hour before Jenny, who has been looking so hard at her mother, that Anna is forced to meet her eye, prompts her with a nod. Anna makes a little 'I know' face in return.

"Look Mum, if you're not going to tell her, then we will", Jenny starts. Emma shifts uncomfortably in her sear, and pours herself the last of the coffee, although, and she knows it, it is stone cold by now. Jenny ploughs on

"I'll tell her then, shall I? Someone's got to. It's not fair on her. Aunt Luce, Mum phoned us last night."

"Yes, I know. I'd just arrived. So?" Lucy looks at the empty coffee pot, then at Jenny. What's not fair on who?

"No you don't understand. She phoned us back afterwards."

"Afterwards? You've lost me. After what?"

"After what you said about Mum moving in with you – sharing the cottage.".

Lucy is bewildered. She toys with her wedding ring, all she has really got to keep of Nigel.

"So your mother rang back. May I know why exactly? I'm struggling to keep up here."

Before Jenny can say any more, Anna places a restraining hand on her arm.

"I'm afraid it's the cottage Lucy. Such a strange thing. I havn't known what to make of it. It makes no sense, but well…….it's not yours, yours and Nigels, not officially".

"What? What do you mean? Of course it's ours. Have you all gone mad? Been in the family for years, you know that. It's our home, where we live. What are you talking about?"

Anna glances at Emma, then at Jenny who nods encouragement at her.

"I'm sorry Lucy. I know it sounds bizarre, and after all this time. It's been years since he and Stella………but apparently, Clive left the cottage to me. There was some problem with the will, a bit missing. I don't really understand. That's why it took so long to……"

Lucy thinks she must be dreaming. None of this makes any sense. She asks Anna to repeat what she has just told her, and then Jenny to reiterate. Her head is beginning to hurt at receiving messages she doesn't understand, can't interpret. Eventually she manages to speak.

"But it's been in the family, my family for years" she repeats, knowing her voice sounds whiny, desperate. "Why would he leave it to you? I don't get it. Are you sure? How do you know?"

"I had a letter, ages ago, years. It was when Phillippe was becoming so ill. I didn't understand, couldn't think about it then. Didn't seem to matter. But now, I suppose, I've got to deal with it – do something about it."

"Do something about it? Like what? Lucy's voice had risen an octave.

"I don't honestly know." Anna stretches her hand out across thee table towards Lucy.

"I'm so sorry Luce. This must be an awful shock."

Lucy wants to pull her hand away, but she doesn't. She feels foolish and embarrassed.

"Don't worry about it – just one of those things, I guess. One of life's unfathomables. I'll need a bit of time to get my head around it – isn't that what people say these days?"

Silence – except for a fox crying up on the cause. The women sit on round the table waiting, waiting for the moment to be gone..

Le Lavandou.
France.

Dear Lucy,

I have been thinking of you constantly since you left, and how you must have felt, be feeling. I wasn't going to tell you, you know. I have a nice home here, and the cottage, well, you grew up there, didn't you? I didn't need it.

Does it sound patronizing if I say, you could have gone on living there, you and Nigel indefinitely? I thought if I told you, about Clive's letter, it would make things awkward between us.

That of course is exactly what I was trying to avoid, but when you asked me to come and share the cottage, I didn't know what to do.

The girls have been pressing me to tell you, so it's been a bit of a bone of contention on that front. I know you've invited them often, and they never go. I could never understand why. They're fond enough of you.

Anyway, please don't let's fall out about this. The girls say you've moved out already. Where are you living? Have you gone back to the flat? You didn't need to, not straightaway. Maybe we could have worked something out.

I'm thinking that you may be right. Now Phillippe has gone, and the girls say they are settled in England, that I should perhaps think about coming back

Please write and let me know your thoughts. You know you're practically family to me.

I'm sending this to the cottage in the hope that it will be forwarded on.

Lots of Love
Anna.xxx

CHAPTER NINETEEN

"Six months before I can see the dogs and the cats – quite ridiculous. How can anyone be expected to make a home without their pets?"
Anna is unpacking boxes of books and stacking them on the book shelves. The book shelves aren't big enough. Anna has hundreds of books.

"Oh Mum, Don't fret. Six months will fly by," Jenny says squinting at the spine of an ancient looking book. "What's this?"

Anna looks up briefly. "Trois homes dans un Bateau. I've got the English version here somewhere."

"Mum, do you really need all these books?"

"Of course I do. Books pets, what home is all about, or it is when your children have grown and flown, and your husband's...."

Jenny crosses the room and puts an arm round her mothers' shoulders.

"It must be hard for you without Dad," she says.

Anna sighs, smiles at her daughter and pats her hand. "It certainly is, but I've just got to get on with it. How about a cup of tea? This unpacking is thirsty work."

Jenny follows her mother into the kitchen.

"Did you hear anything from Auntie Luce? You know after her visit?"

"Not a word. Doesn't seem to be answering the phone either. I've tried the flat, her office. She hasn't been in touch with you then?"

"Nope, not a dickie bird which is strange, or maybe not, under the circumstances. She used to ring up every so often, ask us over."

Anna turned from pouring the boiling water into the teapot.

"You never came here though, did you?"

Jenny opens the larder door and scans the shelves for the biscuit tin. Her mother is still looking at her.

"Why, why did you never visit them?"

"Jenny pops her head back into the room. "Well you know, Uncle Nigel – bit of a perv. Got any cake?"

"He never did anything, did he? I mean to you or Emma?"

"God no. Just let him try. Have you got any cake?"

"Jenny! In case you havn't noticed I've been a bit busy lately – moving house not to mention, moving countries. I havn't had a lot of time for baking."

"Well you might have bought one."

Anna looks impatiently at her daughter. "Well, I didn't. You'll just have to make do with biscuits, and count yourself lucky."

Jenny makes a face at her mother, and they are both giggling, as they gather up the tea things and Jenny leads the way into the sitting room. Anna puts the tray down on the low table, and looks up at Jenny.

"Jen, you would tell me wouldn't you, you know, if anything...."

"What? Uncle Nigel? Nothing to tell, he's just a sad old git." And I shouldn't worry about Auntie Luce, Mum. If she wants to sulk about this place, let her. Life's too short." Jenny plops down in an armchair hugging the biscuit tin, and Anna pours the tea.

CHAPTER TWENTY

"Hi, it's me. You heard from Trevor?"

"Two guesses."

"Oh bummer. Look, why I rang is, well, obviously to see how you are, but also, and you'll never guess...."

Jenny, drily. "Nothing would surprise me. But try."

"Well, it's Aunt Lucy – I've had a letter, or rather, we have. It's addressed to both of us, and to us in our maiden name. but for some reason, she sent it to me."

"Of course, to good old stable Emma, not like me eh?"

"Don't be like that. Anyway she won't know anything about that. You're fine now, aren't you. It was only a blip and Trevor is coming home now, at least to the village. It wasn't your fault, him going off like that, and Mum and everything – enough to push anyone close to the edge."

"Glad you said close as opposed to over. I'll be fine, as long as I keep taking the tablets, eh?"

"Don't be so hard on yourself. They were only to get you through the worst. You'll be fine."

"Hmm, well, thanks for that. Anyway, what's Lucy want then?"

"Well, it's a bit bizarre really. She says, and I quote. "Would it be all right for her to move back into the cottage because Nigel has run off with a schoolgirl!"

"That last bit doesn't surprise me. Let's hope he's gone for good this time – revolting old man."

"Maybe Aunt Luce is exaggerating a bit. You know what she's like, but the cottage bit. Now that really is weird. I know we havn't kept in touch, so she doesn't know, but we didn't know where she went, did we?"

"It's her who hasn't kept in touch Anyway, it's not as if she's our real aunt, though I suppose she may as well be. She and Mum were always so close, more like sisters. But, not a word since that half hearted hospital visit, not one word."

"Oh I know, but what do you think? I can't just not answer, can I?"

"You couldn't, I could. Anyway, how many times did Mum try to contact her after that fiasco in France? She didn't even bother to answer Mum's letters. She was worried sick. For Christ's sake, Em, just write back and tell her no. What else? The bloody place was sold ages ago now, years – long out of our hands, thank God. There was always something funny about that place. Sounds as though Luce has gone off her rocker or something, lost the plot. Seems to be running in the family. Well, you know what I mean. I know she's not family. Maybe it's just age or something".

"You meant Mum then, and Gran?"

"And don't forget the one before that – great Grandma – they all went gaga So we have no chance."

"Don't say that. Don't even think it. And anyway, Mum is still only in her early sixties, and she didn't go gaga, as you put it.. Granny and her mother were well into their eighties before they lost it."

"But they'd probably been going that way for ages."

"Not for twenty plus years though, surely Anyway, you've said it yourself. You have to expect old people to lose their marbles eventually it's natural Everything else starts too give out, break down – physical things, so the brain's bound to give out sooner or later."

"Probably sooner, in my case."

Don't be daft Jen. That was just a blip, I told you. Everything got on top of you, that's all, what with Trevor messing about like that, and then you losing the old place – a right fiasco."

"So you don't think I've got senile dementia, or alzheimers just yet?"

"Course not, and neither did Mum, not when she was first taken into hospital.. Sure she was vague, scatty, forgetting things, but I still think there was more to it than that – something, I don't know what, but something happened there.

Anyway, about Aunt Lucy, and this blessed letter. I won't phone, though she asked me to, some London number, address I've never heard of. I'll write, bit cowardly perhaps, but easier that way."

"Good. Well, let's hope that's sorted then. Did you get to see Mum?"

"Yep. Funny though. One minute she was asking me when she was going home, and looking all sad and wistful. That was when I was trying to explain to her about her having to comer back to Bodmin for a bit, you know, for her assessment. Shouldn't have bothered. Next minute, she was making sort of weird jokes, said that when she lost her sense of humour, we could put her down."

"Gran always said that to her, I remember I was talking to her about Gran, the last time I went, and how difficult it must have been for her, looking after us, and keeping tracks on Granny, you know, when she began to go do-lally. Remember how she escaped over the hospital garden wall, and they caught up with her helping herself in Woolies?. You must remember Em. Poor Mum was always having to jump on the ferry, then the train up to London. Selfish old woman. She wouldn't move nearer, make things easier for Mum."

"I don't remember Mum complaining I do remember Gran coming out to France once, and having too much wine – had us in stitches. Funny, isn't it, how you forget the bad bits when they're gone, and then you miss them."

"Yeh. Fool yourself it was all good bits."

"But that's OK isn't it? Remembering the good bits?"

"I wonder what Lizzie and George will remember about me."

"Bit like the first stage of love, I suppose. Then, when it's over, you only remember that first wonderful bit, and forget what made it not work."

"What would you know? You've been lucky. There's only ever been Jo, hasn't there – since Madame Puquet's class? You've never had your heart broken, have you?"

"It's not just men that can break your heart, you know."

"Well no, in your case, it could be anything from an RSPCA advert to Rosie being upset at school."

"Wouldn't you be upset if you thought Lizzie or George were being bullied at school?"

"I'd go and sort it out before it came to anything. No messing."

"Not everything can be just sorted out, just like that. Look at Mum."

"Yeh, I know. So what are we going to do now?"

"Best wait, I suppose, until after the assessment, something concrete from the doctors. They won't be letting her out to live on her own, or even with us now, I shouldn't think."

"You offering?"

"Jen, it's not going to happen. I did think, at the beginning, that it was just some sort of nervous breakdown, but now...."

"Just a nervous breakdown?"

"You know, something that could be treated, cured I thought, stupid now, I know, that she would get better, just need to make a few changes in her life, you know, sort out what was stressing her, start again."

"Well that's not how it's turning out, is it?"

"No," Emma sighs. Silence for a few seconds. "Better go, phone bill, and all that."

"OK sis. See you. Good luck with that letter."

CHAPTER TWENTY-ONE

Lucy stumbles out of the taxi, clutching her coat, and wrestling with her handbag, and various carrier bags. Her cases are still in the boot. The taxi driver has opened the boot, and is peering round at her, waiting. He thought he had seen and heard everything in his thirty years of taxi driving, but this woman. She really is something else. She has talked almost non-stop from London to Cornwall. He's a chatty man himself, a pleasant, genial taxi driver – gets good tips – makes the customers smile, laugh,– usually Today though, he has lost his sense of humour along with his own ready smile, somewhere between Honiton and Exeter, completely ran out of steam. But she didn't seem to notice, this mad woman. He could probably have said nothing all the way, just nodded here and there – could have saved his breath.

Thank God, they've arrived. He has a nasty feeling though that the end of the fare isn't necessarily the end of the encounter. What if she can't pay, has just taken him for a ride? He smiles to himself now, at his little pun. His sense of fun is never far from the surface, his sense of humour just waiting in the wings – until he can drive away from here, his taxi, nice and empty. He'll stop on the way, give Peg a ring. She'll laugh out loud about this one. So will he, probably – but later.

But for now, what the hell is she doing? The rain which started lightly as they approached Cornwall is getting heavier. It's getting dark too, and the wind is getting up. He turns up his collar, and starts to pull the heavy cases towards him. Why hasn't she opened the front door? Standing there, staring at it like that.

"You all right love?" he calls encouragingly.

Lucy seems startled. She looks back over her shoulder, as she rummages in her bag.

"Er yes, of course. It just looks a bit different, that's all." She turns to smile, apologising for keeping him waiting. "Such a long time since I've been down. You couldn't?" Lucy holds out the key she has retrieved from her handbag.

"Just a sec." The taxi driver swings one of the larger suitcases up and out of the boot and lugs it up the path. It is a very old one with no little wheels on the corners. He stows it on the bench in the open porch.

"Now, let's have a look at this then." He takes the key from her. It's big, slightly rusty, old fashioned.

"Blimey! How long you had this?"

Lucy smiles up at him, giggles a bit as she shifts the weight o-her handbag from one shoulder to the other.

"Oh, as you can see, for ever. We both have one, er, my sister and I."

"Welt you won't be getting in with this. I'm afraid", the taxi driver tells her with a sinking feeling in his stomach. He knew she would be trouble, just knew it. "This 'ere's a modern lock see. You want one of those little keys, you know, Yale or something' like that."

"Oh" Lucy seems unfazed. "Oh well, never mind I'll just have to ring one of my nieces. Don't worry, they'll come and get me, find the right key. There's sure to be one, probably hidden somewhere."

"You got a mobile then?" the taxi driver asks her. She doesn't look to him as though she would know how to use one. Dotty as you like, this one.

"Oh yes, yes of course," Lucy answers brightly, patting her bag. "Hasn't everyone these days?" She laughs.

"Well, what do you want to do? Do you want me to unload the rest of your stuff here, take you on somewhere else, or what?" he asks Well, he has to. No choice. Wouldn't be right, just leaving her. He groans inwardly. She suprises him though, by delving into her handbag, and taking out, not a mobile phone, but a wad of notes.

"This morning you said two hundred. Is that enough? And something for yourself." Lucy pulls another forty from the wad. The taxi driver can't help but smile as he takes the money and stuffs it into his back pocket. But still he hesitates.

"Right, well" he says at last. "If you're sure, I'll get the rest of the cases then."

Lucy doesn't speak, just nods as she sits down heavily on the porch bench looking at the front door as if expecting it to open any minute. The hall within would be cosily lit. There would be laughter, and welcoming hugs. Now she turns her head to smile vaguely at the taxi driver, surprised to see him still here, as he puts down the last of the cases, and walks off down the path. He slams down the lid of the boot, and climbs wearily into the welcoming warm and cosy interior of his cab... He raises his hand in a half wave, although Lucy isn't looking, and drives off into the bumpy darkness of the track.

CHAPTER TWENTY-TWO

A fox barks plaintively across the moor, but Lucy doesn't hear it. She is uncharacteristically calm. She is home, at last, and she is staying. She retrieves the big old key from her handbag, stares down at it, and then at the door with its' tight little lock. It is getting darker by the minute, she should be inside. With a sigh, she gets to her feet and sets off round to the back of the cottage. She knows her way – she should do. Or does she? The back door seems to have metamorphosed into a window. She must have forgotten, been a long time after all. She's not worried – not yet, but stands back to look up at the back of the cottage, what she can see of it, tries to get her bearings, then begins to feel her way on and around towards the kitchen door. But she trips, runs out of path, falling down onto a hard and unforgiving surface where she remembers soft, springy lawn. What the hell, she thinks, is going on? she is sure she is in the right place, and Anna hadn't said anything about altering the garden. They had both loved it just the way it had always been, as Lucy remembers it.

Lucy gets shakily to her feet, not nearly so confident now. Standing motionless in the gloom, she doesn't know which way to turn – literally. Right or left? Does it really matter anyway? She is very cold now, tells herself to think, just think, get back to the porch, get something warm from one of her suitcases. Come on girl, she chivvies herself impatiently. Just move.

Like someone blinded, Lucy stumbles back the way she has come, feeling her way carefully around the cold stone walls until she comes to a window, no, it's a door, a glass paned door. How could she have missed it? She feels for, and finds a cold metal handle. She ties to push it down, pull it up, but it won't give.

"Bugger! Sod it!"

Lucy picks up a stone, the biggest she can find, and pulling her cardigan sleeve right down, and over her hand, she smashes one of the glass panes, gingerly puts her hand through, and joy of joys, she feels a key in the lock. It turns smoothly for her, and at last she is in, standing on thick carpet, warm.

I'm sorry Anna, about the glass, Lucy thinks. But you knew I was coming. Don't I always come down at this time of year? We both do. Lucy can't remember the last conversation she had with Anna. When was it? What did she say?

Lucy crosses to the door, which she can just make out on the other side of the room, and hopefully a light switch, and for the second time goes flying off her feet, ending up sprawled in a tangled heap.

She is furious now. She crawls around the edges of the room muttering and swearing to herself in what is now almost pitch darkness. It isn't easy, there seems to be pieces of furniture everywhere. Reaching the door at last, Lucy crawls up towards the handle, her hands splayed searching for a light switch.

"Bloody hell, Anna. Have you gone mad? What is all this? It's horrible." Lucy is looking around herself in amazement, wondering if she is actually in the right house, but she knows she is, must be. She glares around her at the chintzy sofas and curtains, the coffee tables dotted everywhere, bloody things.

She needs a drink. Drinks cupboard – used to be one in here – always. But not now apparently. The kitchen. Must be in there. She steps tentatively out into the hall, closing the door carefully and silently behind her. Silly, she is aware of that, smiles to herself. There is obviously no-one else here – not yet. The hall looks as she remembers it, almost and except for the nasty red carpet and the wallpaper. Well, things like that do change, don't they?

Lucy opens the kitchen door, gets that right. Gone is the old range, the dresser, the lovely comfy old armchair which was always full of cats and cat hair. Everything looks, is spanking new – fresh out of the showroom. She sits down self consciously and uncomfortably on the edge of a pine bench. She is suddenly very ill at ease, fearful, all confidence gone. What is she doing here? Why?

Well, I can't stay here. Sorry Anna. This isn't home. I wish you'd told me, explained. I could have been prepared. Like the letter. If I had been prepared, well, I might have…….No, no, don't think about that. You must have imagined it – maybe dreamed it. She is talking to herself, but not out loud, but she glances over her shoulder anyway. She gets up and goes to stand with her back to the only clear wall, and even that sports a shiny radiator painted blue to match the walls. The radiator is slightly warm. Lucy starts to open the cupboards. She feels like a burglar.

Crockery, glasses. All anyone could need, but where is the food, and more importantly right now, the drink? She peers into every cupboard and drawer, and even the fridge. Nothing. Ah, she thinks, of course, the freezer – might be something to eat anyway. But no, the freezer is humming away to itself, but freezing nothing. Waiting to be filled perhaps. Lucy leaves the kitchen in disgust, crosses the hall, and wearily climbs the stairs, hauling herself up by the banisters.

CHAPTER TWENTY-THREE

It is six twenty in the morning, but Lucy doesn't know this, won't until she finds her watch which she has left in the bathroom. She lies heavily still, muzzily wondering whether she is awake or asleep still, in a dream perhaps. Wrapped like a mummy, hot stiff and uncomfortable, she half listens to the birds. They sound different this morning. Of course – she's not at home. Different birds, different songs. She's away somewhere. A holiday? So where, and why can't she remember? She is disorientated, and she has yet to open her eyes. She does so slowly, reluctantly, sits up tentatively and attempts to disentangle herself from the duvet. Why does she have to keep waking up? Getting up? What's the bloody point?

She gets slowly out of bed and stands unsteadily beside it. She catches sight of herself in the mirror on the pine dressing table. She almost starts at the sight of the crumpled old woman looking back at her. How did she turn into a crumpled old hag? When? Ah vanity! She needs to clean her teeth, take a shower, or a bath, eat something, drink something. So much to do always. She is so damn tired of it all, hopes every time she performs some everyday task that it will be for the last time, but it never is.

Lucy sits down on the edge of the bed keeping her gaze away from the heartless mirror. She is trying so hard to remember – what she's supposed to be doing – even who she is. She knows she is very hungry, unusual for her. Suddenly she remembers Goldilocks, last night. There was no porridge on the table then, so there is little chance of any now, unless Anna is already downstairs, making it. She always was an early riser, that one. Maybe she is downstairs cooking porridge, making toast and a pot of tea. Yes, that must be it. Lucy feels better suddenly. Then a slant of a thought Last night! What was that all about? Must have had a bad dream. She had a long journey yesterday, didn't she? Well, long for her these days.

Lucy looks vaguely around the room for her toilet bag, doesn't remember having it here. Must be downstairs. She leaves the bedroom in her crumpled clothes from yesterday, then hesitates at the turn on the staircase. Surely, she thinks, there was a window here, wasn't there? Not much of a one, but still. Yes there was, a funny, flimsy little window which looked out and straight down into the garage. It had never opened, but it had been there, always. She fingers the smart new-looking wallpaper, but there is no join, no sign of there having been anything there, just an expanse of papered wall.

Lucy carries on down to the kitchen, but she's not feeling well. Her mind is racing, and she's struggling to keep up. Why does it say these things to her? She wishes it would just be quiet, still. She opens the door to the pristine kitchen, which is empty, and silent except for the humming of the freezer and the ticking of a wall clock. No porridge, no Anna, no nothing. She carries on out through the back door, and round to the side until she reaches the garage. It is open-ended, not thatched like the rest of the cottage. Although it is attached, there is no adjoining door. Apart from a ridge of windblown leaves piled up at the entrance, it is completely empty. Lucy chews at her bottom lip, hesitates for a few whirling seconds, then walks slowly in, and over to where she knows the little window used to be.

The only tell-tale sign, hardly noticeable to anyone who doesn't know for sure about the window, is the white newness of the square that once was a slightly misshapen little metal window. It has been bricked in, and very carefully painted over.

Lucy turns around to survey the empty space. In her father's day the garage had always been full to bursting, with one or two old black, always black, bangers, nose to tale, the second one more out than in.

Those old black cars had not become classics in Clive's day, just bodged up old bangers.

Just behind where Lucy is standing, below where the little window had once been, had stood her fathers workbench. Clive had called it a workbench, and Lucy, not being old enough to know any better had called it that too. Later on though, if, or when she thought about it, and she often did, she knew that it hadn't really been a workbench at all – not a proper one anyway. More likely, it was just something cobbled together from some old doors, or something Clive had picked up by the road or somewhere.

Clive had kept his old chest out here too, the one he had had out in the Far East. It had belonged to Andrew, his father. It was big and greying black with the word ABADAN written in large letters exotically across one side Lucy's friends thought, or was it only Lucy, that it was very exotic. ABADAN! The word had always stirred Lucy's imagination, conjuring up visions of deserts, sand dunes and camels – Lawrence of Arabia stuff. Not that the young Lucy had heard of Lawrence of Arabia until she reached her teens, and then she saw the film three times in a fortnight, and everything fitted in somehow. Maybe the 'workbench' had actually been the chest, and the actual working bench surface, just an old door or panel. It hadn't been very comfortable to lie on, Lucy remembers now.

The little window had been at an awkward height, both for the cottage and the garage, and it didn't open. You couldn't see through it either, not properly either way, but it had been quite useful for tapping on – lunch is ready, that sort of thing. Not that Clive ever took any notice, always arriving five or ten minutes after Lucy and her mother had sat down hungrily to eat, remembering their manners – dare they forget them, and waiting for him to appear.

CHAPTER TWENTY-FOUR

Lucy stands, hands heavily by her sides, motionless. The clouds of memory fly grey and fragmented across her mind. Now they've gone – just evaporated into the air. She can't catch up with them, pull them back, examine them, and why would she want to? All that pain. Now, nothing in her mind, just a blankness so she stands still and waits. It happens a lot, she is aware of that, this standing still, apparently alive, at least on the outside. But she is dead on the inside, as if her spirit has gone out for lunch, or somewhere, left her alone for awhile.

Feeling like some sort of ghost, she leaves the garage and makes her way slowly down the back garden path which runs alongside the garage wall. She passes the laurel hedge, where the path disappears into a muddle of weeds. She picks her way around the bigger, and the more prickly ones. Just discernible is a dirty bramble-covered wall topped by a rusty, corrugated iron roof. The annexe. Lucy knows this place. It used to serve as a playroom on wet days. Somebody used to play house here. Lucy did, and Anna, occasionally, and someone else, but who? It was Nigel, but Lucy can't remember him right now.

The annexe is made up of two adjoining rooms, with a single block bathroom, and a small kitchen tacked on the back.

Battling her way through the undergrowth, Lucy reaches the once white painted door. It is peeling and the handle is hanging off. Lucy gives the door the best shove she can manage, it squeaks painfully and scrapes on the stone floor. Lucy tries again, pushes a little harder. Just room for her to squeeze through. There's not much to her these days.

Inside is a mess, a dirty, smelly mess. There are sheets of newspaper everywhere, enormous cobwebs, dust and dirt. The cottage may have had an overhaul, but the annexe had been totally ignored – almost forever it seemed, tucked away, out of sight behind the overgrown laurel hedge.

Lucy feels comforted. Nothing inside has changed; she recognizes things. The old armchair beside the stove is just as she remembers it. She crosses to the open doorway and peers into the adjoining room – the bedroom, at the big old bed, its' striped mattress yellowed and smelling of damp. Lucy tries to open a window, first in the bedroom, then after no success, the one in the main room, before she remembers, and she does, that these windows never did open, not properly, not in her day though surely they must have opened once upon a time.

Lucy walks through the enormous cobwebs which cling to her to her hair and her clothes to get to the bathroom with its' metal framed windows, painted shut long ago, and its' rust-stained bath. Lucy shudders, then suddenly smiles, as if greeting an old friend, as she turns the taps on and watches the brown water glug and spurt before it falls in a steady trickle, and begins to run clear. Reminds her of something, but what, who? A boy was it? Playing boats in a stream. A nice boy, or was he?

"This'll do me" Lucy speaks out loud. Then, to herself "Just 'till Anna gets..." She stops in mid thought, cocks her head, can hear a strange whirring sound, but she can't make out where it's coming from. She goes back into the living room, and squeezes out of the door. Stepping outside, she listens intently. The whining is almost inaudible now, but she can still feel its' strange vibrations.

Lucy walks round to one side of the annexe, but she can't get around this way for the brambles, big, thick-stemmed, unchecked for years, brambles which cling to, and cover the walls up and beyond the broken and rusty guttering. She tries the other way, but she can't face doing battle again with the brambles and the ivy which seem to be attempting to devour the little building. There is blood on her hands and arms, her clothes have been snagged and torn. Stepping backwards, almost into the laurel hedge, her head cocked to one side, Lucy stares at the old building, holding her breath, listening hard. She can hear it again now. Stepping through a gap in the laurel hedge, she notices a small gate to the side of the cottage garden. It looks new, out of place and time. The gate opens easily and quietly, and Lucy steps through it and out onto what looks like a footpath which runs downhill towards fields and open heathland. The whirring is getting louder and louder.

As she approaches the first field gate, Lucy spots them. Windmills, over twenty feet high. A notice on the gate warns her to keep her distance from the wind farm, informing her that she should follow the footpath around the circumference of the field before the one on which the thin white giants stand embracing the blue sky, and then to take the footpath on and out across the heathland. The whirring is really loud now, not deafening, but invasive. Lucy counts the windmills, as she seems to count everything these days. There are eleven, but three are motionless. Lucy doesn't want to go any closer so she turns on her heel, and walks briskly back the way she has come towards the cottage. Once there, she stands hesitating shyly outside the French windows. She takes a deep breath, and then she finds herself once more in the smart little house. She doesn't like it. She needs to hurry, gather up her things before she is discovered. She takes some other things she might need, soap, bedding. Anna won't mind. She will understand. And Nigel? Well. Who cares what he thinks? Lucy doesn't. Not any more.

Lucy carries everything over to the annexe, going back and forth three times, four times, five times, or is this the sixth? She carts bedding, catching it on branches and brambles, a lamp, a radio, toilet rolls, and once everything is in the annexe, Lucy makes her den.

She is nine years old again, and playing house, the most fun she has had for longer than she can remember. But this Lucy is on her own, somewhere. She has no food, nothing to drink, except water from the tap.

She will have to go shopping. Stella was always sending her down to the shop, alone, or with Anna, for a pint of milk, or bread – yes, Lucy remembers doing that quite clearly. She rummages for her handbag which has become half buried under a pile of damp, musty cushions and pillows in the armchair, and goes out into the lane. She looks up at the sky – still the brightest blue. Won't be dark for ages – she's got time.

The village? Was there a village? Lucy can't remember, or was it just a shop? And which way was it? Right, thinks Lucy, it's to the right. But after walking for ten minutes, she runs out of lane, sees only moorland ahead, miles of it, brown bogland blending into the bases of grey, green hills. She turns and walks back past the cottage, and on until she comes to a crossroads and a signpost. Lucy sighs with relief. She is already getting quite hot, and she could do with a cup of tea. Has she eaten today? She can't remember. The signpost is illegible, and pointing in one direction only, so Lucy follows it, carrying on until she comes to a junction and another signpost. This one though, is covered in moss and mud, and is lying broken in a wet grassy ditch. Lucy leans on the signpost weighing up, or trying to weigh up which way to go, although she has nothing to go by. Should she go right, or should she go left? She hasn't the faintest idea where she is.

"Oh well, the road not taken, and all that". she mutters to herself, and turns right. She walks for almost half an hour, with no sign of any kind of building, let alone a shop. At last, through a break in the hedge, Lucy spots a straggling farm, very run down, but there does seem to be a farmhouse, and a tractor standing in the yard in front of it. Lucy keeps to the lane, resisting the urge to take off across the fields, and is rewarded around the next bend beside an open gateway, a large sign advertising fresh eggs for sale. On the other side of the gateway is an old wooden table on which there are bunches of flowers in jam jars, bundles of herbs, and boxes of eggs. The price list is faded, and there is a rusty old tin with a slit in the top, which rattles halfheartedly when Lucy picks it up.

Eggs – I'm going to need more than a few eggs, Lucy thinks. And what about Anna? I must have something in when she comes. She'll be tired and hungry – she'll need a cup of tea at the very least. Tea, milk, sugar.....

Buoyed up at the idea of seeing Anna, Lucy sets off up the short track. Arriving in front of the large, ivy-covered farmhouse, she decides against approaching the front door, and makes her way down a path alongside the house. She reaches another door, and knocks tentatively. Immediately a cacophony of barking breaks out. Lucy steps back. She likes dogs but... There is much shouting of "Get down, get back" and "Get in there and stay" accompanied by the scrabbling of what sounds to Lucy like a pack of hounds, and a lot of shutting of doors.

Lucy wants to turn away, run, hide, but it is too late, and the door is opening to reveal a small thin woman with black darting eyes, reminding Lucy of two little currants. The woman is wearing an old fashioned flowery, and floury apron. Her red hands, what Lucy can see of them are also dusted with flour.

"Afternoon m'dear." She speaks pleasantly, pleasantly enough to encourage Lucy. "An' what can we do for you?"

Lucy smiles timidly and points back down the track.

"I, er I saw the notice, about eggs. I've just moved into the cottage with my friend." Lucy points vaguely across the fields. Right now she hasn't the faintest idea in which direction the cottage lies, or how far it might be from here.

The woman studies Lucy, not unkindly, as if trying to place her. She takes in Lucy's torn clothes and the scratches on her arms. She frowns which makes Lucy even more nervous. Why didn't Nigel come and do this? Lazy boy.

"'ave you dear? An' which cottage would that be then?"

Lucy looks down at her muddy, scratched shoes, her mind a complete blank. The cottage. What was it called? It was just The Cottage, wasn't it?

"Oh er, just The Cottage – you know, the white one. I say your sign about the eggs, but I wondered if you could perhaps let me have a drop of milk, and a small loaf perhaps if you can spare it – save me going into town, all that. So much to do what with just moving in….." Lucy trails off feeling embarrassed and foolish. She feels her cheeks burning. Why has she got to do this? Why is it always down to her? Selfish lot.

The little woman puts her birdlike head on one side still studying Lucy.

"To town you say? That'll take a while, 'specially if you'm walking." She looks, her expression a question, towards the end of the track.

"Oh well, yes. Thought I'd stretch my legs, leave the car at home, you know, after all that driving, and I meant the village, not the town, obviously." Lucy is gabbling, wishing she hadn't come.

"Hmmm" says the little woman. Well, you'd best come in". She stands to one side to let Lucy step into the large cool farmhouse hallway. "Tell you what" she starts, ushering Lucy down the length of the dark panelled hallway and into an enormous kitchen.

To Lucy's surprise, there isn't a dog to be seen, nor even heard now, but there are dog baskets and hairy beanbags dotted around the room. Lucy loves dogs, always has, is disappointed. Anna has two lovely dogs – she hopes she will bring them with her when she comes.

"Tell you what" the woman repeats. "If you like to sit down, have a cup of tea, I could do with one myself – all this baking. You could take back one of me pasties – they'll only be a few more minutes. Here, you sit yourself down." She motions Lucy to an old blue painted chair at the table. Lucy obediently sits. All the strength, whatever there was of it, seems to have seeped out of her. She is tired and very confused. Is she dreaming, or is she awake, and just wishing that she was sleeping? She tries to keep her head up, and her eyes open. She opens her mouth but she can't speak - can't remember her lines. She looks desperately around for something, someone to prompt her, but it doesn't really matter, because the little woman who introduces herself as Ros Trembell is talking nineteen to the dozen, as Lucy's mother used to say. But what is she talking about? Who is she talking to? Lucy tries to tune in. Something about potatoes, and pasties, the weather, and now, the expected influx of visitors. Lucy takes a very deep breath- tries to calm herself. After all, all she really has to do is smile and nod, here and there.

Roz Trembell sets a mug of tea down in front of Lucy, and Lucy's eyes immediately fill with tears, but the other woman seems not to notice as Lucy dabs furtively at her eyes with her sleeve.

"That all right for you m'dear?" she asks, not looking at Lucy, but turning away towards the oven.

"Lucy sniffs and clears her throat."

"Er, yes, it's lovely" she manages to breathe, and it is. Just to be made a cup of tea these days. She drinks it all straightaway, hot as it is, and feels it warming her, and bringing her back to some sort of present.

"Now then, save you goin' into town this afternoon, or the village, like you said, not that you'd find much there why don't I make you up a little parcel, sort of picnic like, just to get you through tonight."

As she speaks, Roz Trembell is half in and half out of a cupboard, speaking over her shoulder.

"A few teabags – can't do without they, bit of coffee, milk and... oh I know what you can 'ave. I've got a nice loaf in the freezer, not my own of course. I just keeps one shop loaf in there just in case like. I'm not always up to baking me own some days. Oh, an' you'll need a bit of butter. She turns, her arms full of jars and packets. "Make our own we do. There's no many can say that these days".

Roz Trembell places everything on the table before darting out of the room. There is a burst of barking and whining from somewhere in the depths of the farmhouse, then silence as she comes back clutching a polythene- wrapped loaf of bread She busies herself packing an old wicker basket which she has produced from under the table.

"There. You can return me basket next time you'm over this way."

"Oh thankyou. You're so kind", Lucy breathes, eyeing the loaf hungrily. "I'll bring it back tomorrow."

"No rush dear. Like I said, when you'm passing. You must 'ave a 'undred and one things to do." She smiles at Lucy. "You there on your own, did you say?"

Lucy can't meet the woman's eye, but looks down at her lap where her hands are tightly clenched, the knuckles white.

"Oh, just for now, yes. My nieces will be down in a day or two, I expect, and then there's my sister." She mumbles. She thinks, why doesn't she ask me? Why won't anyone ask me if I'm ok?

"Well that's good. Not very nice being out in the wild end of nowhere like we are, not on yer own. Oh, them pasties 'll be done be now". She crosses to the enormous, chipped cream Aga, and opens the hot oven door from which she pulls a tray of perfectly crimped golden pasties. She places them carefully on a cooling rack, except for two which she wraps in two separate brown paper bags.

"That's one for now, and one for, well, when you like."

"How much do I owe you?" Lucy asks awkwardly.

"Oh, get away with you. Tis only neighbourly. S'pect you'd do the same for me, wouldn't ee?"

"But I'd never have to, would I, thinks Lucy. Someone like you would never need my help. You've got a proper life – not like me.

"Thanks, but really, I couldn't."

"Go on with you – 'tis nothing."

As Lucy gets to her feet, now reluctant to leave the cosy, homely kitchen, and set off on her own, Roz Trembell presses the basket into her hands, and opens the kitchen door. At the back door, Lucy turns to speak, but a hand on her arm stops her.

"Now don't you go saying thankyou all over again. You'm very welcome, been nice meeting you. See you again, I'm sure. Bye then." She watches Lucy walk down the path, noticing as Lucy bends forward to close the gate, a thick lock of hair which has fallen down to obscure her vision. Lucy has to put the basket down, and tuck the hair firmly behind one ear before she can continue.

Lucy seems to come to as she turns from the gate looking about her. She can't remember which way she came. She didn't actually say goodbye, and did she say thankyou? She hasn't a clue – cannot remember. She walks very slowly away from the back of the farmyard. The basket is heavy, and she is unsure of where she is in relation to home. Should have brought Nigel with her, or better sent him. He would know exactly which way to go. She walks aimlessly at first, then she thinks she recognizes a clump of campions, and then, more reassuringly, she spots the signpost sticking almost mockingly out of the ditch. She fancies she sees the top of a bus in the distance, but nothing appears before her in the lane, no bus, no car, no-one.

"Nobody came because nobody does" she mutters to herself. Who said that? So familiar, and yet.....

At last, her back aching mercilessly, Lucy comes to a cottage. It looks familiar so she puts down her basket and gazes at it. Such a pretty little place.

Feeling as though her arms are about to break, Lucy reluctantly picks up the basket, and walks on past the cottage, turns up the footpath, and uses the gate in the hedge to reach the annexe. She pushes her way in, and closes the door as tightly as she can. But it won't shut so she has to put a chair against it, and even then it is still ajar. There is no bolt, no sign of a key, and anyway the lock is broken, rusted away with time. The handle is surprisingly good on the inside, so summoning the last bit of strength she can, she wedges the back of the chair under the handle. Nice and safe. Safe here.

She decides to make herself tea and toast. Might be a very long time until supper She can't start before Anna arrives. She is very hungry though, too hungry, and so tired, that lured by the saggy old armchair, and the aroma of the pasties, instead of going into the kitchen to make a cup of tea, she drops down into the chair making the dust billow, and herself sneeze rib achingly three times.

With the basket cuddled on her lap, she cannot resist taking out one of the pasties, and tucking into it – just what she needs. Then she is gobbling, bolting it down, the lovely, not too greasy, just moist pastry, the steak, the potatoes.

It is delicious, but Lucy begins to feel full before she is halfway through. The pasties are big, and maybe she isn't as hungry as she thought. She rewraps the uneaten half, and stuffs it back into the basket – she'll finish it later. Nigel might like it anyway, while she and Anna are preparing supper – always did have a good appetite, greedy man.

Lucy rests her head on the back of the armchair, not even registering the bristly stuffing spilling out. She closes her eyes and falls into an exhausted sleep. But it doesn't last.

Waking abruptly less than twenty minutes later, Lucy is, frozen and stiff. She is disorientated, and very frightened. Where is everyone? She looks around the murky room. It is almost dark. Where is she? What is she doing here? She feels the heavy bulk of the basket pressing down on her stomach. Where is the kind old woman? The one with currants for eyes. She sits quietly feeling the panic course through her, and subside a little before even trying to get to her feet, get her bearings. Anna. Yes, that's it – Anna. She's waiting for Anna.

It is getting darker by the second. Lucy gets slowly and stiffly to her feet, and forces herself across the room to try the light switch. She doesn't have the energy to hope that the switch will work, but it does, and the shabby room is suddenly transformed, almost into cosiness by a pinky orange glow. There are no curtains to draw though, and Lucy looks at the old woodburner imagining it's warmth. "Never mind" she says more briskly than she feels. "Nigel can sort that out – job for a man. Where the hell has he got to? He's very late home tonight?"

Lucy takes the basket into the kitchen, but can't be bothered to unpack it now. She glances out of the window, imagines she sees the lights of a car, heaves a sigh of relief. But there is no car. She stands motionless, feeling the time moving on around her, past her, and without her.

She should go and start making beds, put some towels out – that sort of thing. She would like an early night really – pity she has to wait up for other people. She can still taste the pasty. It's not lying too well –too fresh, she thinks, like fresh bread, hot from the oven – always did give her indigestion. She stands at the window, peering into the darkness, her arms crossed. Her upper arms are as cold as ice. Why doesn't Anna come? And why hasn't she phoned, she is so very late. Not like her not to phone. Lucy glances down at her wristwatch frowning in the dimness of the kitchen. Her watch says a quarter to eight – but when? Morning? Evening?

What time did Anna say? She tries to imagine Anna saying a time, making the arrangement, but she can't get her, can't picture her or hear her voice. Clenching and unclenching her hands, Lucy tells herself to relax, settle down in the armchair and just wait. At least she will be doing something normal while she waits, sitting down, having a sit-down. She sits, stares down at the floor, but she isn't seeing it.

Tea. A cup of tea. That tea was nice; she'd like another cup like that. Perhaps when Anna arrives they will have a cup of tea together. Lucy smiles to herself. Just have to be patient, that's all. She leans her head back, closes her eyes, and is gone again through memories and dreams to weird dreams of people she doesn't know, in places she has never been.

Exhausted, run down like a flat battery. Even in the depths of sleep and dreams, Lucy sees herself – a battery that can never be recharged, but thrown away, replaced.

She can't wake up, can't get back. She begins to struggle against the dreaming, and the dragging sensation that is pulling and pushing her down and down.

CHAPTER TWENTY-FIVE

"I'll get him." Anna bounds up the stairs to the funny little corner on the landing. She breathes hard on the panes of the tiny window. She starts to rub at the murky glass with her sleeve. Well, it's not that dirty. Something makes her stop in mid rub just as she is about to tap on the glass, make a funny face, mouth 'cup of tea time'. But she doesn't tap. Clive is there, but he hasn't noticed her. He is looking down at something. He is smiling, almost bent over the workbench. Anna has never seen Clive smile like that before. What is he doing? She can't make it out. She steps back from the window unsure what to do next. Standing side on, afraid she is interrupting Clive, and that he will be annoyed with her, Anna looks down again. There's Lucy now. She can just see her, sort of, her blond hair hanging over the end of the bench. She's lying on the bench. But why? To Anna the tableau below her made no sense – at first. Then, a funny, fuzzy sick feeling surges through her. She stands frozen, her hand still half covered by her sleeve, now not to tap, but to stop herself from crying out. She mustn't be seen.

Anna turns away from the window, her legs suddenly like jelly. She forces them to carry her back downstairs.

"Is he coming?" Sheila asks, over her shoulder, as she butters bread. "Cake's in the tin. Put it out, would you dear?"

Anna moves towards the larder, shrugs her shoulders, hopes it will pass for a reply. Her feet feel like lead. She doesn't want any cake. She feels sick, but she helps Stella anyway. Between them, they take the tea things out on trays into the garden, place them on the old picnic rug.

"Clive?" Stella calls. "And Lucy? Where has that child got to?"

They both appear, Clive and Lucy, she a few steps behind her father. They are approaching along the other side of the hedge, on the road side, then through the garden gate. Clive opens it, and turns, waits, smiles down at Lucy as he ushers her into the garden, one arm around her shoulders.

The wisps are gathering together like the cells of a tumour, on Lucy's shoulder, smoky grey wisps which will grow instead into a small cloud, at first, before they grow with her, accompany her throughout the rest of her life.

"There you are. What have you been up to?" Stella asks, glancing at Lucy as she pours tea, and hands it round, not expecting an answer. Ask a silly question....

CHAPTER TWENTY-SIX

"Jenny, it's Mum. Grans' had another turn. They think this is probably it, so I'm going up to Northampton........ Yes, tonight...... Well, I'll get the sleeper. A bit extravagant, I know....... No you won't, I can manage. ......No, no need, she wouldn't know you anyway.... No, she hasn't known who I am for a couple of years now.... No, it's OK....... Yes, course, I'll be fine...... Could you phone Emma and tell her?..... I will...... Bye Darling, yes bye."

Anna quite enjoys the sleeper, fresh white sheets, waiter service. Maybe I could just live on a train, she muses, as she dozes off in the surrealism.

It is too late. Her mother has died, having been unconscious for several hours. Just didn't wake up, slipped away, the nurses said. Best way to go. They were sympathetic in a busy sort of way. Happens all the time – business they're in.

Anna signs a few forms, picks up her mother's personal bits and pieces and arranges for everything else to go to the charity shops. She puts up in a hotel nearby from where she goes to visit, the undertaker and the local vicar.

"I do them all dear," the vicar says. Anna finds this piece of information less than comforting. But then, she tells herself when people die at Tall Trees Residential home, they are without exception, ancient and mindless.

"Such a sadness," The vicar says looking suitably, but to Anna, surprisingly sad.

She feels that perhaps she should apologise to him for her mother's death –upsetting him like this.

"Don't worry, my dear." The vicar says brightening, and clasping Anna's hand as she leaves. Between us, Donald, the funeral director, you've met him, such a nice man, and those lovely people at the home. We'll sort everything out, nothing for you to worry about – probably the end of next week. I'll give you a bell. Ha"

The vicar laughs at his own little joke, which Anna hardly recognizes as such. She hopes her mother can cope with all this attention. Still, she thinks, as she walks back to the hotel, Mother's long gone. I bet as soon as the last breath left her body, her spirit was off like a whippet – free at last.

Anna decides to stay at the hotel for another night, go home in the morning. She phones Emma. She buys herself a bottle of wine, and after an early supper in the hotel dining room, she settles down in her room to sift through the two small cases of her mother's personal papers and possessions.

Anna takes a sip of wine. Does she feel like doing this tonight? Yes, may as well, might be able to chuck some of it, lighten her load for tomorrow. According to the nurses, even until the last, Mary had guarded these two cases, not allowing anyone so much as a peek. From the difficulty Anna had prising open the lid of the little black one, it seemed as though not even her mother had opened the case for a very long time.

The case is crammed with paper, letters, forms, envelopes, old receipts. God mother, whatever have you kept this lot for? Anna sips her wine and starts to go through the receipts most of which are dated the year before she was taken into the home. May as well chuck these, surely.

Anna hesitates. Maybe not, maybe she will just take them home, sort through them at her leisure. The girls could help. Might find something interesting amongst the piles of paper.

Anna closes the black case and hauls the smaller blue one off the chair, and on to the bed beside her. This one opens sharply. Inside, more papers, but in neat elastic banded bundles. Letters, personal letters. Another job for another time, Anna decides, picking the bundles up anyway, and flicking through them with her thumb. At the bottom of the case is a long brown envelope. It makes Anna's heart jump because it has her name written clearly in large letters on it, and it is sealed. In the top left hand corner in red ink, it says private and confidential.

Anna puts all the bundles of letters back in the case and closes the lid. Then she opens it again, maybe there are letters for other people. But there are only the bundles of opened envelopes, nothing else. She closes the case, puts it back on the chair and settles back against the pillows with the letter addressed to her. She takes a gulp of wine and tears it open. How does she feel? She couldn't say.

Her mother's familiar handwriting, clear, perfectly punctuated, not the spidery scrawl of her mother's last years. She glances at the top of the letter to check the date, but there isn't one.

My Darling Girl,

Anna feels a lump rising in her throat. This is mum, she thinks, this is my mum, not that dotty old lady I've been visiting for years. "Hello Mum", she says to the letter.

I hope you are reading this, and no-one else. It should be you., and only you. I have to tell you something which in all honesty I have felt it better for you not to know. I did not feel that it would be in your best interests, neither did your father. We were trying to protect you – from confusion, from hurt.

I know you always looked on Clive as, well, a sort of uncle or father figure. Well, he was always there, wasn't he? You were so little…………

Anna feels a niggling pain starting in her chest. She sits up hoping to dislodge it, but it persists. She turns the pages of the letter over. There are three pages. She reads the last one, again and again and again, until her chest hurts so much, she can hardly breathe. Tears well up but stop short of falling. Cry? No, think, think, try and work it out – a jigsaw puzzle that's what it is, she thinks, just a jigsaw. I can do it. It will make sense. She puts the letter down on the bed beside her, inches herself forward and swings her legs off the edge of the bed. Wine – she needs more wine. She finishes the bottle; she wants more.

She wants oblivion. She crosses to the small fridge next to the dressing table. Drinks taken from here will cost double what she would pay if she just went downstairs, but...

She drinks the miniature brandy, and the whisky, and the small bottles of red and white wine.

Sitting on the floor, she finishes the packets of peanuts from the fridge door. She tries to get to her feet. She reaches out for the dressing table stool, but it doesn't help her up. Instead, it topples over and hits her on the nose. She crawls sobbing to the edge of the bed and after several abortive attempts manages to pull herself up, and collapses face down on the quilt.

CHAPTER TWENTY-SEVEN

Anna sits silently in the back of Jo, her son in laws car. She sits, not squashed but comfortably cosy between Jennifer and Lizzie. Lizzie is the only one of the great grandchildren to attend Mary's funeral. The others are busy living their lives – no need for them to come, Anna has said, much to the youngsters' relief. But Lizzie is able, and willing to get away, to escort her mother..

Everyone is quiet even Lizzie, sensitive to the atmosphere, just looks out of the window.

Anna woke in Emma's spare room this morning. They would be able to make an early start in the morning, she and Jo thought. Jenny and Lizzie had stayed too.

It was a black morning. Anna had pulled back the curtains and been disheartened by the pathetic attempt at the spring morning sky which only seemed to turn the blue patterned bedroom curtains into two black, blank walls like long hair hanging down either side of a gothically white face.

So, no morning glow from God today, nor any attempt by Mother Nature to demonstrate her powers. The day, like the curtains threatened to merely hang there, not a breath of wind giving any lift or lightening to the budding trees. Perfect day for a funeral, Anna had thought wryly as she dressed in her black suit, the same one she had worn to Phillippe's funeral, not so long ago.

As they speed through the counties, the sky lightens a little. Not bright clouds in a grey sky, but the gaps in the greyness giving an impression of potential brightening.. It is the grey which is cloud, thick, wide with only the odd irregular break in the strips of gloom sliding past the window, an illusion only.

As they leave the church and walk slowly the short distance to the cemetery, someone switches on the lights. The sky moving across the wispy tree tops of the churchyard silhouetting and prettily illuminating them – a pale greeny brown, almost golden hue. The white uplight comes not from a bright sunray, but is nevertheless an uplifting presence. A breeze is getting up now, as the coffin is lowered, light but playful, it mixes the branches up, criss crossing them, bringing them to life. The mourners turn to smile sadly at one another, then slowly make their way back to their cars and their own journeys through life.

They drive home – all in a day. No wake for Mary, but a sandwich and a drink in a village off the motorway. The pub garden is pretty. A spaniel puppy lolloping about claims Lizzie's attention. Jo and Emma and Jenny are talking quietly. Anna looks up at the sky. Proper clouds now. Fluffy white ones against a blue background, just above her, yet on the horizon, grey tufts too – a messy old sky after all. The light has dimmed again and the silhouetted branches looking only black now, wild, wintry almost, bleak and depressingly leafless. But it is Spring, there should be buds, leaves. The wagging branches seem to be pointing at Anna, or are they beckoning to her like evil witches fingers?

Anna shudders, tries to concentrate on eating her sandwich, but it won't go down. She is very cold.

"Shall we go Mum? Not having any more? Are you O.K?" asks Emma, taking her mothers arm and helping her to her feet.

Anna takes her daughters' arm, but she can't look at her, can't speak. It is as if her spirit has left her body in the care of some half spirit, like one of Emersons' half gods, a not very efficient spirit, one who doesn't have Anna's best interests at heart, her own worst enemy in fact. This feeling is not new to Anna. It has happened before, and it is happening more and more frequently. She feels herself being pushed out of bed onto her feet in the mornings, and propelled without encouragement into the day which she is becoming mote reluctant and ill equipped to manage.

"You all right Mum?" Emma gets up and taking Anna's arm in hers guides her towards the car park. "I think Mum's getting cold. We're going back to the car. Don't be long," Emma says quietly to the others as they finish their sandwiches and beer, and Jo gets up and goes inside to pay.

CHAPTER TWENTY-EIGHT

It is nearly six months since the funeral. Anna is standing in her nightdress, her eyes only inches away from the protective shield of the curtains. It is early. She turns her head to look at the dishevelled bedclothes unsure whether she finds them inviting or repellent. She finds them neither. It is just a good place to hide, that's all. She could curl up under the rumpled duvet, pull it right up over her head and pretend she wasn't there any more, sort of stop – stop everything, just for a while.

Anna feels that that is what she needs – just not to be for a while – give herself a break, time out. Stop the world, I want to get off and all that. A trite clichéd joke, but must be what people like her, if there are any people like her, think when they want time out, extra time, double time even. Perhaps what she really means, really wants is to become double herself. One of her could stay, carry on, function seemingly normally, whilst the other could go, just leave, recharge in some other place, some other time.

Anna opens the curtains a fraction, prepares to squint at the light, but it is such a dull, light, if you could call it light, light for winter possibly, but even as she looks at the trees, everything is darkening. The branches look black, wild wintry, depressingly bleak and leafless, their bony, black twiggy claw like fingers pointing, poking at her, admonishing her.

She pulls the curtains back together, cutting out the accusing witches fingers. She can't be held responsible. Why her? It isn't her fault.

Shivering violently, she gets her dressing gown from the tangled heap on the bed, wraps it around her. She is cold, so very cold.

She stands between the window and the bed, then sits down heavily on the edge of the bed. She could go and make herself a cup of tea. That would be functioning wouldn't it? Making tea is something to do, a normal everyday activity, not a task, not really. Because it's for her though, it feels like a task, a chore. If she thinks about it any other way, it is pure self indulgence, and that won't do. But everyone does it, don't they? Hundreds, probably thousands of people, men, women, capable children, the length of England, are putting on kettles, popping tea bags into mugs or teapots, standing gazing out of kitchen windows, some more alarmed than others at the possibilities or probabilities of another unfurling day.

Tea. Yes. Do it, just do it, Anna tells herself. At least start the process. One thing leads to another. Before you know it, you'll be under the shower and after that, Oh God, after that, you will stand at the open wardrobe and worry, really fret about what to put on. Where are you going today? Anywhere? Who will you see? Anyone? Or, will you just hide out here – see no-one? Usually best. So, jeans? Dirty, garden stained ones, or in case you do go out, or someone calls, ones?

Anna decides to dress now, immediately. She cannot face repeating the thought processes she has already put herself through. She gets as far as her knickers, then stands in front of the mirror hating her mutilated reflection, her badly matched breasts.

Shouldn't matter really, not now – not at her age, but it does. It just does. She wants to be able to take things like that for granted, matching breasts – wouldn't any woman?

She peers hard at the reflection of mount Vesuvius to the left of her chest, and the fried egg to the right. Mount Vesuvius appears to be attempting to disappear under her left armpit. The reconstruction, more complicated, obviously, than the actual mastectomy, had involved taking a strip of flesh and muscle from her back. Perhaps this strip of her body knows this that it is in the wrong place and is trying to make its' way back.

Sad loyal little fried egg just clings on, not even plum like any more. Still at least it has a nipple – one between two. Of course, (why of course?), it didn't lie between her breasts but was placed exactly where it should be, had always been, in the centre of her flat little white breast. So that's nice.

CHAPTER TWENTY-NINE

The Grange Residential Home for the elderly is situated equidistant between Jenny's house, and Emma and Jo's farm – perfectly placed for regular visits from both Jenny and Emma. Not only is it extremely handy, it is also very nice. Nice as in well run, comfortable and prettily situated at the end of a country lane with views over open farmland to the woods beyond. The staff, all local, are kind, efficient, and seem genuinely fond of their charges. Arrive at any time of day, and there is music playing, laughter, and a relaxed atmosphere.

Anna likes it here – quite. It's not home, wherever that is, and there's only one four legged resident. Admittedly the enormous white cat does spend most of its' time in Anna's room, but she could do with a dog or two about the place.

Sometimes Emma brings George, Anna's old poodle, to visit, but neither Anna, nor George, although he is very polite about it, appear to recognize one another.

Anna doesn't seem to recognize anyone, anymore.

It is afternoon, and Anna is sitting in the residents lounge. The white cat has wandered off, probably outside. It's a sunny day and he loves to sunbathe and roll around in the dust. He will go to Anna's room first when he comes back, and when he finds her not there, he will come to the lounge and jump on her knee, whether she has visitors with her or not.

Today Anna has visitors. She sees them from across the room as they enter the lounge, two attractive young women, one blond, open faced, the other, older, dark, more wary. Why, Anna wonders, are they here again? She's sure she recognizes them. It's nice that they come to visit. She likes them, friendly women like.... She doesn't want to think about the past though nor the present, and a future no longer features in her thinking. There is to be no more anything.

The two women are smiling hopefully and encouragingly across at her. Anna begins to get wearily to her feet, and this slow, painful to watch action makes them quicken their steps, and almost run, arms out to steady her back into her chair.

"Mum." Jenny leans forward awkwardly, and hugs her mother, then stands back to allow Emma to do the same. "How are you? Are you all right? Are you eating and things?"

"Things?" Anna looks up puzzled. "What things dear? I'm here. I'm well, and what was it? I'm eating, oh yes."

The girls exchange glances. This isn't Mum, but then it never is these days.

They sit down, pulling their chairs in close around the little table, forming a group, a private group in what feels like a very public place.

"Are you taking any tablets, Mum? Have they given you something– you know, to help you sleep, or anything?"

"Tablets? Oh yes dear, lots of tablets. We all have lots of tablets. How else do you think they keep this lot under control?" Anna, a flicker of her old self, gestures around the room where all is calm except for the odd altercation, or cry for assistance. There are men and women all within a similar age group, elderly, but not geriatric, sitting in armchairs or shuffling about.

"Isn't that, you know, he used to run the little Post Office in Witton?" Jenny says nudging Emma.

Emma looks across at the man in trousers and pyjama jacket walking laps slowly around the edge of the room. He is humming tunelessly.

"God, yes it is. Mr er, Hawes or something. Yes, I'm sure it's Hawes. He was always so, well, so nice, seemed O.K."

"Just shows" Jenny mutters.

"Shows what dear?" Anna said looking from Emma to Jenny.. "I should be going home today, I think. Dogs must be wondering where

I've got to, bless them." Anna looks around as if she is about to ask someone something.

"Oh Mum" Emma and Jenny exchange glances. They have long since learned to play the game.

"Don't worry about the animals. You know we've split the dogs between us. Emma's got George and Raffs, and we've got Bess, and the cat's are fine. Lizzie's feeding them, cycles up there every day after school.. Then Trevor or I go and pick her up in the car."

Anna looks blank "Lizzie? I knew a Lizzie once – lovely red hair – gorgeous child. I wonder what happened to her."

Jenny looks sadly at her mother, and Emma takes one of Anna's hands. She holds it gently in hers. It isn't old, gnarled. It is still pretty, just as her mother is still pretty. She shouldn't be here. She doesn't belong here. Tears prick at Emma's eyes.

"Mum, Lizzie's got blond hair. She's your granddaughter – your first grandchild. You remember, don't you?"

Anna turns her head towards the window, looks at the trees. She is gone. She neither moves, nor speaks for ten minutes until the girls lean across, kiss her and get up to leave..

CHAPTER THIRTY

"It's not your baby, I've told you." Mary sobs hysterically. Then, more quietly. "How many times do you want me to say it? I've said I'm sorry, and I am. So, so sorry. What else is there?"

Derek, mild mannered Derek, leans over her until their faces are almost touching, until her tears splash onto his cheek.

"You could do me the courtesy of telling me who has had the pleasure of my wife, exactly whose little bastard it is."

Mary clutches her baby more tightly to her as she watches Derek's adams apple bobbing furiously and ridiculously up and down, whilst the veins standing out in his neck threaten to burst. His face is puce.

He turns away from the bed, stubbing his toe on the baby's cot.

"Blast and dammit," he swears loudly, crosses to the window. He is shaking with emotion, with fury. The baby in Mary's arms starts to whimper. A nurse appears at the door.

"Mr and Mrs Lockett. Please.. We really can't have all this shouting. You're upsetting the other patients."

"Sod the other patients." Derek turns, sneering. "Have they all had their husband's babies? You wouldn't bloody know, would you?" He strides, across to the door, and shoves his face within inches of the nurses.

She doesn't flinch. She has experienced this sort of thing before, but she's not going to tell Derek.

"Mr Lockett, I must ask you to leave, otherwise I shall have no choice but to call security....again." She whispers the last word under her breath, as Derek turns away, his eyes fixed on Mary.

"Are you going to tell me, or shall I put it another way? I shall keep coming in here and asking you until you do."

Mary, believing him sighs, looking down at the baby. She is so tired, but she knows, always has, that this scene was inevitable. There is a lump in her throat now, but she has to, somehow, get the words out – the nurse and Derek are waiting and it will be a relief, after all this time, she knows that.

"I suppose you do have a right to know." She speaks haltingly. "Of course you do, but I don't, I don't want to upset Stella." There is a catch in Mary's voice. "Promise me. Please Derek, none of this is her fault. Please promise me Derek."

"I'll promise you nothing. Why should I -and Stella? It's me you should be worried about upsetting, you..... Anyway, who the bloody hell's Stella?. What, you don't mean Stella next door? What do you mean?"

The penny drops and nearly knocks him out. He slaps his hand to his forehead.

Of course. No, surely not, not Clive, Clive Woodrow, our friendly neighbour" Derek just reaches the chair by Mary's bed before he crumples into a heap. "I don't believe it, and yet, yet, now I come to think of it, maybe I do. It's all becoming clearer by the second". His head drops onto his chest. He hasn't the energy to hold it up. The nurse waits at the door. They don't know it, but both women are holding their breath.

"Clive Woodrow, good old Woody. How long have I known him? Thirty years – you'd think you'd really know someone after thirty years."

He gets shakily to his feet.

"Well I hope he can afford you, because you won't get a penny from me, you nor your brat – got next months mortgage payment put by, have you?"

Mary looks at him but remains silent. She is exhausted, relieved, fearful, but it's done now. Let him rage, he's hurting. He doesn't mean it..

"And don't think I don't mean it." He goes to the door. The nurse stands back to allow him to pass.

He walks quickly away down the corridor. Stella will never hear those footsteps again.

CHAPTER THIRTY-ONE

"Just look at those two – could be sisters. Look at the way their hair falls, and their profiles. They really are....."

"Huh! What? You mean them two? Hardly. One's an old sweetheart, and the other's as mad as a box of bloomin' frogs, and a right old b....."

"Tracey! That's not fair. How could you? She's only been here five minutes, and anyway, you should know better than that."

Elaine, ward manager now for more years than she cares to remember, wishes she had kept her observations to herself. The young seemed to have no time for the old these days – no interest. Elaine glances again at the two elderly women, heads bent forward toward each other.

Anna Du Bois wears a velvet alice band which keeps the bulk of her surprisingly thick hair back, but a curl at the front is forever escaping. The other old lady, Lucy something or other, had only arrived a couple of weeks ago when Elaine had been off. . Lucy's hair is short, mannishly short at the back, and quite straight, except for a stubborn little tuft at the front which looks poised to curl if left to grow long enough.

"What have they got to talk about anyway – been like that all morning," says Tracey, grumpily pushing her mop under a chair. She'd like to put a pillow over their toothless old mouths – the whole blooming lot of them.

"Move your feet, there's a love," she says to the occupant of the chair who is fast asleep with her mouth open. Tracey gives the old slippered feet a shove with the mop, gently, so that Elaine doesn't notice. Tracey hates her job, cleaning up after these nutters, and not one of them under seventy. She'll get down to the job centre later – find something else. Must be something less bloody tiring.

Afternoon now. No Sheila, just Elaine, and a couple of nurses, and auxiliaries. Visitors come and go – it's open house most afternoons. The doctors have long gone, done their ward rounds off to play more interesting ones on the golf course.

Outside the open french doors, the inmates and their visitors sit at tables on a sunny, paved patio. The area is surrounded by a shoulder high wall, high enough presumably to deter all but the very determined, and tall, escapee.

Anna has no visitors today –her girls are busy, though hardly girts anymore, newly released from the daily domesticity by the absence of their children away at university, abroad, who knows where? Not Anna. And anyway, she has a new friend to occupy her. Lucy sits opposite, her turning her face to the sunshine.

"You'll get old and wrinkled before your time if you do that. Bad for you, the sun." Anna says, frowning at Lucy.

Lucy turns her old and wrinkled face to Anna, and chortles.

A nurse appears from indoors bringing a tray laid with cups and saucers and a plate of buttered scones. Both old ladies look up at her, eyebrows raised, questions in their eyes.

The nurse puts down the tray.

"Biscuits? You can have biccies as well. That it then, girls?. O K then. Just for you."

Both the old women beam happily at her, though neither speak. The nurse turns back into the ward calling,

"Biscuits Clance, out there, for Anna and Mrs Steele."

A muffled reply follows, and a plate of biscuits is brought out to them by a chubby cheerful girl called Clancy. She has a ring through her eyebrow.

"All right Anna?" she says, putting a plate of plain biscuits down on the table.

"Nice to see you back here again."

Anna looks blankly up at the girl.

"Lizzie?...."

"Lizzie! Lizzie who? No, it's me, Clancy. You remember. I was here the last time you came. And the time before, come to that. How you doing – that home, the Grange isn't it? What's it like there then?"

Anna stares blankly at the girl, then an expression of vague realization flutters across her face.

"Oh, The Grange, yes dear. Well, it's lovely, a lovely hotel, sea views, everything you want. Been going there for years. It was time for a change though, and I do prefer it here, friends here,,,"

"Here! Really? Crikey! Clancy turns away and disappears indoors.

"I knew a Mrs Steele once, I think," Anna says, sipping at her tea and smiling at Clancy's departing back. "She wasn't called Clancy though." They both nibble their scones and sip their tea appreciatively. Their eyes meet over the rims of their teacups, seemingly full of affection and complicity.

A tall old woman with a brown spotted, whiskery face, shuffles out of the open glass doors and makes a beeline for Anna and Lucy. She is oddly dressed – a lime green crimplene dress over navy nylon trousers all under a loose tunic in vivid pink. She stops behind Anna's chair and taps her on the shoulder. Anna jumps.

"Anna's eyes widen with fear as they dart from the woman towering above her, to the dark interior of the ward. She wants Elaine to come. Lucy just stares blankly up at the woman.

"There you are Joan. Come along now. Mustn't bother the ladies."

A nurse appears and takes the whiskered old woman gently by the arm, and guides her back indoors.

"Outside with your slippers on? Whatever next?" she chides the old woman. Joan allows herself to be led away.

"But my appointment, my dear. You don't understand. My car is completely blocked in. It really is too bad."

Joan ducks and twists her head to look the nurse full in the face.

"Could you just ask them dear – to move it?"

"Yes Joan, of course." The nurse assures her patting the old ladies hand as arm in arm they cross to the bedrooms. "We'll see what we can do eh?"

Milton Keynes UK
Ingram Content Group UK Ltd.
UKHW020229250424
441687UK00001B/84